To Fonda!

Gene Frap

May 2018

A secret alchemical recipe to transmute copper into gold surfaces in first-century CE Caesarea. As soon as Miriam sets out to trace the leak, Judean terrorists target her for assassination. Eluding the assassins while protecting a secret of her own, she discovers that she, herself, is responsible for the leak. Moreover, she is powerless to stop its spread throughout the Empire and beyond.

But who is really trying to kill Miriam? Is it a case of mistaken identity, or is her late fiancé's ex-scribe, now an assistant to the procurator of Judea, seeking to avenge an old grudge? Or is her heartthrob's half-brother, a Judean patriot who inherited his mother's mania, afraid Miriam knows too much?

And how did the recipe find its way from Alexandria to Caesarea anyway?

Also by June Trop

The Deadliest Lie

The Deadliest Hate

by

June Trop

Bell Bridge Books

⊰B

Bell Bridge Books
PO BOX 300921
Memphis, TN 38130
Print ISBN: 978-1-61194-667-3

Bell Bridge Books is an Imprint of BelleBooks, Inc.

We at BelleBooks enjoy hearing from readers.
Visit our websites
BelleBooks.com
BellBridgeBooks.com
ImaJinnBooks.com

10 9 8 7 6 5 4 3 2 1

Cover design: Deborah Smith
Interior design: Hank Smith
Photo/Art credits:
Hieroglyphs (manipulated) © Diego Elorza | Dreamstime.com
Gold texture (manipulated) © Wyoosumran | Dreamstime.com
Silhouette of ancient city and guardians © Vyacheslav Biryukov | Dreamstime.com
Two architectural columns on a white background © Timonko | Dreamstime.com
Grecian Woman © Winthrop Brookhouse | Dreamstime.com

:Lhdx:01:

Dedication

For my Paul

"From the deepest desires often come the deadliest hate."
—*Socrates*

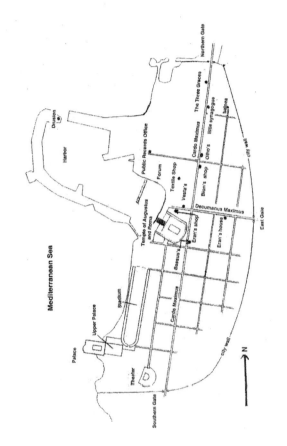

Caesarea

Mediterranean Sea

Adapted from Netzer (2006)

Used with permission

The Eighth Year of the Reign of Tiberius Claudius
Caesar Augustus Germanicus [Claudius]
48 CE

Part One:
Alexandria *ad Aegyptum*
Three Weeks Before the Summer Solstice

Chapter 1

Late Morning

THE CORNERS OF Phoebe's lips trembled as she handed me the wood-framed tablets. She'd been cradling them in her arms as if she were carrying a baby.

"Miriam, the jewelers' courier just delivered this letter for you. It's from a goldsmith's shop in Caesarea."

Phoebe was the foundling my mother rescued from the *Bruchium* quarter, the palace area of Alexandria. But over the years, she's become more than our family's beloved servant. Five years my senior, she's become a big sister to me.

She'd rushed into my sitting room in the private wing of the first floor of our family's townhouse in the Jewish quarter. One of the maids had just cleared away the remains of my breakfast of dates, almonds, goat cheese, and a wedge of wheat bread flavored with cinnamon, but the aroma of the tea she'd made from wild mint and elderflower still perfumed the air.

As soon as Phoebe said Caesarea, I knew the letter had to be from Judah. He'd sailed to Caesarea last September to find his half-brother, Eran. Judah learned he had a half-brother only two years ago when his mentor, Saul, a master jeweler and Eran's father, confessed on his deathbed to also being Judah's father.

When I touched the tablets, it was as if I could feel the heat where Judah's hands had been, a sensation that triggered that dormant but familiar longing that was both pleasure and pain. I caught my breath and closed my eyes to conjure up the image of him I muse on before falling asleep. He's standing in his shop as he did that first day when Papa sent me to the agora to collect his mortgage payment. When I walk in, I see his lids lift, his pupils widen, and I hear the rhythm of each breath slow and deepen to a sigh.

In the inky darkness of my *cubiculum*, relieved by only the softer darkness that floats in on the moon-cast shadows of the cypress trees outside my sitting room windows, I intoxicate myself with Judah. First I concentrate on his broad shoulders and narrow waist, his rugged cleft chin and high-bridged nose, his luminous green eyes, and the glossy black curls that frame his brow. Then I re-live the feeling of having been near him, of my pulse quickening and my flush mounting as I fill my lungs with his air, a hint of sandalwood riding on a heady male scent like honey on freshly-baked bread.

I rose from the cushioned mahogany sofa of my sitting room and walked around the marble-topped wicker writing desk to bring the tablets into the trapezoid of light the morning sun had painted on the mosaic floor. Then I broke through Judah's seal, untied the leather bands that bound the hinged tablets, and opened the leaves to their waxed surfaces. Eager for any hint he might regard me as someone more than a comrade in the League of Alchemists or the friend who'd bathed his dying father, I scanned the letter for any tender phrases.

There were none.

I curled my hand around my neck to check the rising blush of mortification for daring to believe he could love me.

Phoebe asked, "Is he all right?"

I just shrugged and perused the letter quietly.

The beginning was ordinary enough.

The Shop of Eran ben Zahav
May, three days past Calends
The Eighth Year of our Emperor's Reign

My dear Miriam,
I found my brother right here in Caesarea. He calls
himself Eran ben Zahav. I am staying in his home on
the Decumanus Maximus *one block from the East*
Gate. His goldsmith shop is on the same street just
south of the Forum. Caesarea is a city like

Alexandria, prosperous, cosmopolitan, and a center of Greek culture with the usual monuments, statues, and baths.

He continued in this vein, writing about the sights in Caesarea and his pilgrimage to Jerusalem for the Passover. But the next paragraph rocked me like an uppercut to the jaw.

Something about Eran bothers me. He's been bragging to me about having a recipe to make a certain product, the very product Saul and I tried so long to synthesize. But he won't tell me how he got the recipe or what it says.

Judah knew I'd recognize his reference to the formula he and Saul had been developing to transmute copper into gold. What's more, he knew that any allusion to such a formula would be too dangerous to put in a letter. What he didn't know was that the news would howl through my belly like a cold wind.

I'm disappointed that Eran would think I'd steal the secret to make a fortune at his expense. Even if Saul and I hadn't been developing our own recipe, the last thing I'd do is steal it, especially from my own brother. And, of course, I'm astounded that others had been working on that same procedure and curious about their methods.

I too was astounded, but unlike Judah, I was more than curious. Everyone knew the copper would first have to be blackened, and then the deadened mass would have to be heated in a bath of mercury. But no one other than Saul and Judah could have thought to seed that bath with beads of gold.

And then the following paragraph knocked me out.

So, I'm sorry he won't discuss the recipe with me. From the little I've gleaned though, it sounds like the one Saul and I formulated. But, of course, that would

3

*be impossible. I know the notes were never out of
your or my possession.*

The guilt from that blow twisted my entrails because the
notes actually had been out of my possession, albeit for less than
a week. Two years ago on Shabbat, three scrolls had disappeared
from my cubby in Papa's library: my design for an apparatus to
vaporize and condense metals safely, the League's copy of
Aristotle's *Meteorologica*, and most important, Saul and Judah's
recipe for the League, a process to perfect copper into gold. I'd
lied to Judah that Sunday when he'd been expecting me to return
them. I told him I'd simply forgotten them and would return
them in a week, the week that ended up almost costing me my
life.

Having lent them to me without Saul's permission, Judah
was annoyed, impatient to get the scrolls back before Saul noticed they were missing. But I knew he'd be stung to the quick
had I told him they'd been stolen. Still, more than to keep
Judah's yellow bile in balance, I lied to keep from losing face
with him and of course, but to a lesser extent, to maintain my
status with the other alchemists who were still debating whether
to accept me as a full-fledged member of the League.

And the blow choked me with dread because I feared that
Judah and Saul's notes were at that very moment flying through
the aether ready to provoke accusations that we Jews were conspiring to debase the emperor's currency. The Almighty had
entrusted us, His Chosen People, with His Divine Art, charging
us to protect His Lore from the ignorant and the vulgar, and I'd
sent His Secret aloft on the wings of Mercury to incite, G-d
forbid, another pogrom.

I'd been eight years old when the Pogrom of 38 erupted.
Papa told me we had to stay within a tiny sector of the Jewish
quarter, or we'd be killed, that frenzied mobs using stones, clubs,
swords, and fire, were looting our shops, stealing our property,
destroying our synagogues, torching our homes, and forcing our
women to eat the flesh of swine. But he never told me what had
happened to our elders, how those who hadn't already been

stripped and scourged in the theater or stoned, pummeled, torn limb from limb, or burned alive in the agora were crucified outside the Gate of the Sun near the hippodrome.

But even without another wholesale pogrom, our comrades in the League could still be charged like common thieves with conspiring to cheat their clients. As a Roman citizen, I could at least appeal to Claudius for the right to defend myself in a proper trial. After that, the worst I could face would be a presumably painless death by beheading. Judah and the others, being non-citizens, would be summarily crucified. Like the vilest of criminals, they'd be left to hang outside the city gates to suffer the *summum supplicium*, the most extreme punishment, after which there could be no burial, no lamentations, no peace, only their wandering souls, the buzz of blue-green flies, and a jackal's marks on their scattered bones to serve as an appalling warning to others.

So I had to find out whether I was responsible for the leak and regardless, to see whether I could prevent the Gentiles from getting hold of our secret. Until then, the nightmarish creatures that haunted me two years ago would own me once again.

Chapter 2

Late Afternoon of the Same Day

"PHOEBE! WE'RE GOING to Caesarea!"

She'd just bounced into my sitting room, swinging the yellow woolen satchel she'd taken to the market. The fringe of dark hair framing her face fluttered as she plopped into one of the occasional chairs that flanks the sofa. As I turned from my desk chair to face her, I saw that the fading afternoon light filtering in through the wide, east-facing windows had gathered on her round, girlish face.

I'd sent her in Papa's sedan chair to Aspasia's apothecary shop for some cannabis leaves that the cook could brew into a tea to calm my nerves. But more than the cannabis, I wanted to rest my forehead against the cool marble slab of my desktop. All of a sudden, my fears of losing Judah—and a million times worse—of provoking another pogrom, were once again clutching at my vitals. I needed to ponder Judah's news and at the same time chase away the monsters of the underworld that were threatening to overtake me.

From her slouch in the chair, Phoebe tossed the satchel with the bundle of cannabis leaves onto the blue jasper tiles that inlay the top of the sofa's cedar end table. "Judah's asked you to marry him! I knew it!" Clapping her dumpling-like hands, her eyebrows shot past the wisps of hair that feather her brow.

"Does this mean we're moving to Caesarea?" Her dimples deepened as her smile widened in anticipation of my answer.

"Heavens, no. And Judah and I are not getting married either." I felt another blush racing up my neck, but I squelched it by imagining Judah's face if he ever found out I'd lied about the scrolls. "Unfortunately, it's more serious than that. Remember when the scrolls disappeared from my cubby in Papa's library?"

"Sure. But you got them back, right?"

Her face puckered with questions.

"Anyway, what's that got to do with a trip to Caesarea?"

"There were secrets in those scrolls, Phoebe, and those same secrets may have surfaced in Caesarea."

I'd been careful at the time to withhold more than Phoebe needed to know about the disappearance and recovery of the scrolls. I certainly didn't mention that Noah had filched them from my cubby. No wonder she leapt to her feet, sprang across the room, and gripped me by the elbows.

Pearls of sweat clung to the fine hairs above her upper lip.

"Oh, no, Miriam. I can't believe we're going to have to track down another set of secrets. Last time, you were beaten and left for dead." Her voice broke, but then she blinked and took a deep breath. "Besides, Judah's already there. Can't he do it?"

"I'm afraid not. I never told him the scrolls disappeared from this very house. I was too ashamed. Worse than that, I pretended they were never lost. If I ask him now to trace the leak of an alchemical secret, his no less, I'd have to tell him why, and that means admitting I lied."

A pall gathered between us.

"Listen," I said to dispel the gloom. "Speaking of getting married, isn't Caesarea where Bion lives?"

"Oh, Miriam. That was so many years ago."

Bion had been a public slave in Alexandria who repaired scrolls in the workshop of the Great Library before being sold to a Jewish craftsman in Caesarea. Phoebe met Bion when she brought him scrolls from Papa's library. As a sideline, he'd repair privately-owned scrolls to earn the money to buy his freedom. He fell in love with Phoebe and wanted to marry her as soon as he could save enough to buy her freedom as well as his own. He wrote her several times from Caesarea, but she continued to refuse his proposal, telling him that free or not, she'd never leave our family. So eventually his letters stopped.

"You're right, Phoebe, Bion was a long time ago, but maybe

we can find him anyway."

"Maybe, but with Judah it's different. You know he's coming back to Alexandria. He loves you, Miriam, and he'll be overjoyed to see you."

Phoebe couldn't have been more wrong.

Part Two: Alexandria *ad Aegyptum*

Two Weeks before the Summer Solstice

Chapter 3

Late Morning into Late Afternoon

"THANK YOU, PAPA. I know you haven't always agreed with my decisions, especially about Judah, but your helping me arrange this trip means a lot to me."

We were in my father's study, a small square room off the atrium. The Etesian winds that temper our summer sun feathered my nose with the fragrance of the roses nodding in our courtyard. My father was leaning back in the armchair behind his massive ebony desk, his fingers interlaced across his belly, one of the peristyle columns behind him casting a faint stripe down his heavy-featured face. I was in my usual position sitting across from him, but I was no longer the supplicant I used to be. I was a full partner in managing our family's investments.

"I'll miss you while you're away, Miriam, but I learned the hard way when Binyamin deserted us and forsook his heritage that I must let my children decide their own future."

My father was referring to that day two years ago when my twin brother, wrapped in his chlamys, a sporty traveling cape, and his Roman self-control, carrying only his Iberian leather travel bag, slipped out of our house and made his way to Capua to train as a gladiator at the famous *ludus* that owned Spartacus more than a hundred years ago. My father was still bitter about Binyamin's departure, especially in light of the deathbed promise he'd made to my mother to give their only son the best education possible.

"Besides, I trust Eli to accompany you and Phoebe until Judah meets you in Caesarea. Before you were born, Eli's father, my second cousin Samson, was a regular visitor to your grandfather's house, but . . ."

True, Samson was before my time, but Aunt Hannah had told me all about his visits. He'd been my blind aunt's only suitor, but my father and grandfather had misgivings about a betrothal.

". . . So you'll set sail in early July, providing the winds are favorable, the pre-sail sacrifice goes well, and . . ."

I'd first heard the litany of omens a captain has to watch out for when Binyamin was planning his voyage to Rome, the first leg of his journey to Capua. Aside from the end of the month and a few specific dates, Roman ship captains identify a gamut of other circumstances that bode evil. Something about a crewman or stevedore sneezing on the gangplank; a crow or magpie perching on the rigging; a wreckage spotted on the shore; a dream of goats (especially black ones), bulls, or wild boars; and a million other portents of disaster.

After reeling off a few more omens, my father got down to his arrangements with Eli. Leaning forward, his brows contracted, a fan of grooves tightening around his eyes, his head nodded as his index finger jabbed the air with each point on his mental list. But the substance was that Eli would accommodate Phoebe and me on his father's ship, the *Orion*. The voyage from Alexandria would take about three days, after which Eli would sail on to Cyprus and Byzantium to establish *stationes* there to expand his father's trade route to Athens.

So as soon as my father explained our itinerary, I withdrew to my sitting room to compose a response to Judah. Taking up my silver stylus, I used the flat end to wipe out Judah's message and the pointed end to scratch my reply into the wax. No doubt he'd be surprised to learn that Phoebe and I would be coming all the way to Caesarea, but I offered no explanation. I simply gave him our itinerary and asked him to listen at the port for the herald to announce our ship's arrival, secure lodging for us in an inn suitable for women traveling without a chaperone, and meet the ship to escort us there.

I had to re-write the letter a few times; otherwise he'd never recognize let alone be able to read my penmanship. I was trembling, and the stylus kept slipping through my clammy grasp. At last I completed the letter, folded the tablets together with their frames overlapping slightly to prevent the wax surfaces from rubbing, re-tied the leather bands, melted a stick of wax across them, and stamped the puddle with my seal.

I sighed as if I'd finished a day's work in the mines.

Next, Phoebe helped me don my himation whereupon I summoned the bearers to take me in Papa's sedan chair to The Pegasus, the inn fronting the *Eunostos* where Binyamin had awaited the departure of his ship to Rome. The *Eunostos*, meaning the Port of Good Return, is the smaller and western of our two harbors and our port for exchanging goods with the cities along the Mediterranean. Surely I'd find a traveling merchant there to hire as my courier. Like all the waterfront inns serving the *Eunostos*, The Pegasus is in the *Rhakotis* quarter, the Egyptian quarter and our poorest district, and like Papa, I'd learned a lesson, namely never to venture into that underbelly of the city alone, even in broad daylight.

The city's colonnades and porticoes, fountains and monuments, sphinxes and temples, statues and palaces glistened in the midday sun as the bearers ferried me past a drove of pigs, a platoon of soldiers, a herd of sheep, and a caravan of camels, all the while casting a thick, swiftly moving shadow of our chair on the one-hundred-foot-wide Canopic Way. Wheeled vehicles are banned from sunrise to late afternoon, but the bearers still had to weave around other obstacles like bronze-fitted sedan chairs and curtained litters, street philosophers, and impromptu orators. Likewise they had to dodge dung sweepers wielding shovels, priests waving palm fronds, whores flaunting their charms, and idlers drinking honey-sweetened water inside dwarfed polygons of shade.

They had to skirt as well the usual eddies of dust, piles of excrement, and lacey pools of spilled henket, the Egyptian beer made from barley or emmer wheat. By pressing my palms against my ears, I managed to muffle the groans of millstones, the clip-clop of hoofs, the call of tricksters, the clatter of foundries, the clang of smithies, the din of tinkers, the squawks of seagulls, the buzz of flies, and a medley of neighs, brays, and barks. But I could do nothing to deaden the scrape of soldiers' hobnail boots and the clink of the metal studs on their leather skirts as they marched across the *Heptastadion*, the causeway connecting mainland Alexandria to Pharos Island. Nor could I temper the reek of the sticky entrails clotted with blood and the stringy sinews threaded with fat that hung outside every butcher's stall and attracted every sort of pest.

We headed westward from the Jewish quarter through the *Bruchium* quarter past the Great Synagogue, the Great Gymnasium, and the Park of Pan. Needles of light poked through the fringed canopy, and wider shafts threw the fronds of date palms into feathers of shade across the shimmering pavement. Then, just beyond the adjoining campuses of the Museum and Great Library, we turned northward onto our other thoroughfare, the Street of the Soma, the bearers loping along, their feet barely touching the roadway as the flat-roofed tenements and gabled townhouses hurtled past me.

We turned westward again through the twisting, cobbled lanes of the warehouse district, its lumberyards, stables, slaughterhouses, and storage bins pressed together shoulder to shoulder. Finally, after blundering their way through the seedy, litter-strewn backstreets around the *Kibotos* or Box, the small, square artificial port inside the *Eunostos*, the bearers crossed over the canal into the *Rhakotis* quarter and through a maze of rutted alleys and gutters to The Pegasus.

Lowering the chair near a sign depicting Pegasus as he sprang from Medusa's womb, the bearers agreed to wait for me while I inquired for someone heading to Caesarea. I picked my way along a well-worn, dust-coated walkway past the street-front bar to the inn itself—its façade is decorated with a mural of Bellerophon on the white, winged Pegasus—and ventured in through a scarred oak door that cut through one of the stallion's wings. A sliver of light accompanied me inside.

The public room was virtually empty save for the ferocious flies. Strewn about the earthen floor and lit by a ring of dying oil lamps suspended from the stained ceiling were wooden tables and benches, some overturned presumably in the diners' haste to leave, understandable given the smells that confronted me. I figured they must have supped last night on rotten fish and rancid mutton washed down with stale henket. Adding to the foulness were the tang of putrefying garbage from the kitchen and the stench of human waste from the latrine. I was appalled that, of all places, this greasy box was the last home my brother had before leaving Alexandria, perhaps for good.

Propped up in the corner on a wooden stool, leaning against a slanted wall, dozed a bronze-skinned dwarf, his weathered face lined with dirt, his chin sunk to his breast, his graying Hebraic beard splayed across his chest. I cleared my throat to check whether he was sleeping deeply, but the sound came out like a gag. In response, his eyelids fluttered, and scratching his little potbelly, he made a blubbery sound with his lips. Then, coughing up an oyster of phlegm, he opened his eyes and spat the slime into the chamber pot below his dangling feet. When he saw my sandals, he started, raised his head, and rubbed his eyes as if to clear his head.

"Blessed be His Name! What's a fair maiden like you doing in a place like this? Or have I joined the World-to-Come?"

The power of his voice and its mellow production of sounds belied his stature and our shabby surroundings.

"Excuse me," I said, "but I'm looking for an itinerant merchant to carry a letter to Caesarea."

"Nathaniel ben Ruben at your service," he said, jumping off the stool, lifting his right hand from his heart to his lips to his forehead, and, with a flourish, bowing deeply from the waist. "I'm to sail on the next Roman merchantman leaving for Caesarea, so I can join up with a caravan headed for Jerusalem. Nowadays even Roman soldiers hiking along the most frequented highways have to travel in force to forestall an ambush by Judean terrorists, who, along with beggars, escaped slaves, and all the other riffraff lurk behind every hill and inside every ravine."

"I need someone to deliver the letter in the care of Eran ben Zahav, a jeweler, about thirty-years old with a port-wine stain across his forehead." I had to stoop to meet his gaze. "You could drop it off at his jewelry shop overlooking the Forum or at his house on the *Decumanus Maximus*, one block from the East Gate—"

He lifted his meaty hands and held out his palms.

"I know the city well, missy, having spent half my years trekking back and forth between Caesarea and Jerusalem."

His weathered cheeks webbed with laugh lines reminded me of Nestor, the produce vendor who'd rescued me from that alley in the *Rhakotis* quarter when panther-eyed thieves attacked me and left me for dead. So, satisfied he'd deliver the letter, I gave him the tablets, which he secured in a leather drawstring pouch under his stool. Bubbling with gratitude and filled with relief, I emptied my purse into his cupped hands. His tattered cloak assured me he could use the money.

With that mission accomplished, I found myself sighing for the second time that morning, but as long as I was out and about, I had the bearers take me to the Bank of Gabinius to arrange for credit at their branch in Caesarea.

Part Three: Aboard the *Orion*

Early July

Chapter 4

Evening of the First Day

"SO, YOU'RE UNCLE Isaac's daughter. My father told me all about your beautiful aunt. I suppose you look just like her." A bead of spit flew out with Eli's flattery.

"Actually, my father—he's prejudiced, of course—says I have my mother's tall frame, fringed eyes, fair complexion, and vigorous curls, but my hair is chestnut whereas hers was blonde."

He sat back, his sidelong glance settling on my breasts as he sucked in the corner of his lower lip. Embarrassed for having called attention to my appearance, I changed the subject immediately to my father.

"I think my father is your cousin, not your uncle, a second cousin to your father and a second-cousin-once-removed to you."

"Whatever." He flicked his hand as if shooing a fly. "My father speaks often and kindly of Uncle Isaac."

Somehow I doubted that.

He seemed to read my mind because he patted down the air with his palms as if to plead for my indulgence.

Eli and I were alone, sitting across from each other on massive carved oak armchairs in the parlor of his suite, one of the lavishly appointed cabins of the *Orion*'s deckhouse, the raised afterdeck for the captain, owner or his agent, and any special guests. On this *corbita*, a wide sailing ship with a rounded, big-bellied hull for cargo, the deckhouse offered the luxury of a banquet room, cabins, promenades, and lounges, all with mosaic floors depicting scenes from the *Iliad*. Aside from Phoebe and me, another guest, Gershon ben Israel, an Alexandrian who imports Palestinian wine, would be traveling with us as far as Caesarea. We'd meet him tomorrow. The rest of the passengers, a never-ending stream of ship owners, bankers, merchants, government agents, public couriers, and tourists, camped with their servants, sharing a tiny tent on the deck.

A blunt-chinned, portly waiter in a long bleached-linen apron was about to light the candelabra and otherwise finish setting our table for dinner. Another waiter, this one weedy, with a parchment-colored face and droopy eyelids, brought us an Oriental platter piled with damp cloths to bathe our face, hands, and feet. Shafts of light from the oil lamps in the corridor streaked the paintings that decked the cream-colored walls, some of which I recognized as sights from Alexandria: the huge basilica of the Great Synagogue rising behind its double colonnade and the Pharos Lighthouse as seen during the day from the mainland entrance to the *Heptastadion*. The tall windows both starboard and port were draped in a double-dyed saffron silk, its vibrant red folds tied back to encourage the mild, brine-scented breeze to float in on the starlight.

Eli was dressed as a Roman but with too much torso for the pigskin girdle about the waist of his short-sleeved, knee-length Attican wool tunic and too little neck for the scarlet Chinese silk *laena* about his shoulders. His stubby fingers either fiddled with the *laena* or toyed with his single piece of jewelry, an iron signet ring bearing an intaglio engraving of a grain ship on a deep red, almost black carnelian stone. His face and the backs of his thick but manicured hands were hairless despite the dark mane foaming about his head, which caused me to wonder how many hours he must spend with his *tonsor* to wax, tweeze, and shave his body and facial hair. I figured by the time he reaches Byzantium, he'll look like an overfed gorilla.

Assuming a stiff, upright position, Eli brandished his fluted goblet, threw back a swallow of pomegranate wine, licked his upper lip, and cleared his throat as if bringing an audience to attention.

"Good wine," he boasted before spraying me with a sour belch.

I let a sip flower in my throat as I gazed at the curios (the antique vases, funerary urns, and prehistoric figurines) in the pair of matching citron wood cabinets that rose from the tessellated floor to the coffered ceiling and bathed the room with their fruity scent.

Eli put down his goblet and drew in a deep breath. "Perhaps you've noticed the distinctive features of this ship."

I gripped the arms of the chair to brace myself for a lecture.

"It's a *navis oneraria*, a ship of burden carrying some 340 tons of grain. My father has a fleet of them in the Indian Ocean, but this one is a favorite of mine, built by a Roman, named for a Greek, but owned by a Jew." Eli forced a chuckle at his attempted witticism.

He continued to boast, mostly about his business triumphs while the waiters served the first course, a soup of sorrel and sage. He interrupted himself only long enough to insist on inspecting the simmering caldron before he would permit the waiters to serve it. I suppose I should have felt flattered. Instead, I began to understand why, if Eli was anything like his father, my grandfather and father might have objected to Samson as a suitor for Aunt Hannah.

Samson had started a trading company to transport goods by sea between the Mediterranean and China. They believed he was more interested in my aunt's dowry than her welfare, that he'd take her to distant cities along his trade route where they couldn't protect her, that he might even leave her there while attending to business in other cities. So they found fault with everything about him, claiming his laugh was too loud, his nose too long, his palms too damp, his cologne too strong, his hair too greasy, his manner too familiar, and his tongue too glib. It took me a long time to forgive my father for depriving my aunt of an opportunity for happiness.

Still, if the truth be told, at this point my father would gladly embrace Eli as a son-in-law given my age, almost nineteen, and Papa's need for another business partner. Amram was just too despondent after the death of his only son, my late fiancé Noah, to attend to their partnership.

As soon as I finished my soup, the weedy waiter hinged his body over the table to remove our bowls—Eli's untouched—while the portly one wheeled in a cart and parked it next to Eli. Its upper tier bore a platter of roasted capons and salvers of brined olives, deviled eggs, and melon balls. No sooner had Portly begun to serve us when Weedy re-appeared, shouldering a silver tray of grilled lamb in a fragrant plum sauce, a salad of wild greens and berries, and a covered dish of steaming cabbage, all of which he unloaded onto the lower tier of the cart.

When Eli plinked a spoon against his empty goblet to signal one of the waiters to refill it, my attention snapped back to his monologue. At some point, he'd changed the subject from the quality of the pepper he ships from India to his view of Judean politics. My interest quickened.

"To the outsider, Judea may seem peaceful, but a festering movement threatens the stability the Romans have brought us. Underground thugs calling themselves Zealots claim to be liberators in the cause of Judean independence, but they're nothing but outlaws foolish enough to challenge the mightiest power on Earth. All they accomplish with their guerilla warfare and agricultural strikes is to stir up hostilities against all Jews and disrupt our opportunities to expand commerce and shipping, the very enterprises that could improve their wretched lot."

He paused to stab an olive with his knife while I enjoyed the short-lived silence and the sweet undercurrents of the salad.

"The Romans have contempt for these Zealots because they won't fight a *bellum justum*. They won't meet the Roman army head on. Instead, cowards that they are, they ambush the lone soldier or Jewish businessman in the countryside—"

"So I've heard. Not even a legionnaire dares to travel alone—"

His eyes flashed at the interruption. In a Herculean effort to stay composed, I focused on the blue vein throbbing at his temple as he continued.

"But fortunately the Romans know how to deal with them," he said while poking the air with his spoon. "Just two years ago, the current procurator of Judea, Tiberius Julius Alexander, captured and crucified Jacob and Simon along with hundreds of their miserable followers. Maybe you heard of these rebel rousers, sons of Judas of Galilee, the founder of the Zealots. Alexander, a Jew himself, mind you, but hated as an apostate even more than as a procurator, doesn't waste time with floggings or beatings. Under his administration, twenty thousand Zealots have already been crucified."

I pictured a highway stretching beyond the city gates, a ribbon winding into the hills, its edges lined with upright posts as far as the eye can see. A grim procession of hundreds of shackled prisoners are marching under the control of a score of granite-faced soldiers. The brass helmets of those in command are crowned with a feathery red crest and flash a blinding light under the scorching sun. Accompanying the prisoners and soldiers are the executioners who, along with their ropes, axes, buckets, and freshly sawed crosspieces, ride toward the summit in a convoy of carts, each lurching in turn as it jounces over the same bleached human skull. Then one by one, the executioners nail the outstretched arms of each condemned man to a crosspiece and haul him up by ropes to face a handful of dusty spectators and a swarm of hungry horseflies.

"Another threat to Roman stability comes from the pseudo-messiahs and false prophets who are springing up everywhere in Judea. But the latest menace may be the most dangerous, a splinter group emerging from the Zealots but one the Zealots disavow for their sheer brutality. Called the *Sicarii*, this secret brotherhood of ruthless assassins is named for the short, curved daggers, the *sicae* they conceal under their cloaks."

A flinty edge had crept into Eli's speech. Spittle gathered at the corners of his mouth, and every now and then, he'd square his shoulders, curl his fingers into a fist, and thwack the table, at which point the dishes would rattle, the goblets would clink, and the table would groan.

". . . They've been organizing terrorist cells in (*thwack*) every Judean city. But more than taking aim against our Roman administrators and bureaucrats, they direct their attacks against their fellow Jews, the ones they say 'bow too low to Rome.'

Unfortunately, they don't mean just the high priests who accept favors from the legion. They also mean us, the 'Greek' Jews they accuse of being faithless collaborators with Rome. But no one, (*thwack*) absolutely no one, has been able to capture them. So they continue to slaughter with impunity. They might waylay their target in the marketplace, and then, before the unlucky corpse has had a chance to bleed out, they're melding with the crowd. Or at one with the shadows and heard only by the wind, they might slip into their enemy's home and leave him with only the swiftness of their blade and the silence of his screams."

I took another sip of wine to quell the frisson pulsing through me.

So engrossed was I with his account of the *Sicarii* that I started when the waiters approached to clear the table for tea and *dulcia domestica*, a chilled dessert made from pitted dates soaked in wine and stuffed with dried fruit, nuts, cake crumbs, and spices. But having no appetite for the rest of the meal, I was relieved when Eli, after lowering his goblet and flashing me a silky smile, levered himself out of his chair (but not before banging his knee on the edge of the table) and offered his arm to escort me back to my cabin.

The night breeze swept the deck, darkening the moonlit surface of the water, whipping the loose strands of my hair, and fanning the cloying odor of Eli's cologne. Aloft on wine and swollen with pride, he resumed his lecture, this time with one arm sweeping toward the ship's tutelage.

"The *Orion*'s guardian deity, essential on the sternpost of every Roman vessel," he said. "A gilded statue of Zeus raising the giant huntsman to the heavens." Pivoting toward the stempost, he continued. "Another wooden figure, this one our insignia, depicts Orion with his hunting dogs." With another sweep, this time toward the hold, Eli explained how the cargo is stowed in layers, something about loading the amphorae of wine and oil first, just above the ballast, and stacking the sacks of grain last, after the building stone, tiles, and ingots. But don't take my word for it. Weariness had already settled into my bones.

When we reached my quarters, I thanked him for dinner but

in a tone distant enough to signal that the evening was over. He excused himself with a nod but only after an uncomfortable pause. I spun around toward my cabin door so quickly I could feel my skirt whip against my calves. Then, in a wash of relief, I listened to his lumbering footsteps fade into distant thuds. His cologne lingered though, as if painted on the walls. I tapped on the stout oak door. With no response, I turned the curly iron handle and slipped inside.

Phoebe was already asleep, purring on the pallet beside my sleeping couch, sweetening the air with her breath. She'd laid out my *capitium*, a short, light chemise for sleeping, and left one candle burning in the candelabrum. I quietly undressed, leaving a puddle of clothes on the cool floor. Then I slipped on the *capitium*, uncoiled my hair, snuffed out the candle, and sank into the bedding.

As I lay there, I imagined Eli at the stadium with his other Romanized friends enthralled by the brutality of the games. At first, they're bored because the gladiators seem to be fighting mechanically as they drag their feet across the blood-soaked sand, but then the younger one loses his footing. Taking advantage of the moment, his opponent thrusts his sword. Eli's savagery awakened, he stands on his seat, craning his neck, drenched in sweat, flourishing his fist, eager to witness the gladiator's death. I hear the crack of ribs, and then, as the victor raises his blood-drenched sword to salute the procurator, I see that the younger one is my brother, lying in the dust, oozing a ribbon of blood as he takes his last breath.

I threw off the vision with a shudder, and then, to fend off a maze of morbid dreams, I focused my thoughts on Judah. I imagined our bodies entwined, his sun-warmed hands bringing my passion to life while I arch my back and raise my knees to welcome his thrusts and dissolve into the rhythm of his movements. When I could no longer stand the excitement, I put my hand where it shouldn't be and muffled a cry of pleasure.

Chapter 5

Afternoon of the Second Day

I WAS SITTING with my feet elevated on a long chaise in one of the deckhouse lounges. Re-reading *The Clouds*, I was amusing myself with Aristophanes's caricature of Socrates when Gershon ben Israel glided into the room to greet me.

"You must be Miriam bat Isaac, the daughter-in-law Amram ben Eleazar hoped for." When he reached for a chair with his impossibly long, delicate fingers, the sun gathered on the face of his amethyst seal ring and threw an oval of light onto the ceiling. "My condolences to you on the untimely death of your beloved."

He was hardly the portly businessman I expected. Instead, he had the stature and loose-limbed grace of an athlete, broad-shouldered and trim except for a ruffle of skin that draped his jowls and a dewlap under his chin. He sat down beside me, arranging his limbs easily. Then he smoothed out the soft folds in his deep blue silk tunic, which he wore just below the knees in front and to the mid-calf in back. When he rested his verbena-scented hands in his lap, I noticed his sheepskin girdle which, like his sandals, was studded with garnets. To complete the ensemble, a gold brooch, set with an amethyst like his seal ring, was positioned on his shoulder to fasten a Greek-style cloak.

"I hear this is your first trip to Caesarea. What brings you to Herod's Roman city?" Angling his body toward me, he spoke in the mellow voice and unhurried speech of an aristocrat. The network of blue veins across his narrow forehead appeared to stitch his cap of luxuriant silver hair (freshly oiled and styled in the latest Roman fashion) to the matching pair of tufts that bounced as he spoke and shaded his intensely blue eyes from the harsh light that seeped between the slats in the starboard shutters.

I looked away to roll up the scroll of Aristophanes and tuck it beside me on the chaise so I wouldn't have to face him when I stated the reason for my trip, but the fib slid out easily enough. "I'm traveling on business for my father. We're interested in buying up small farms in the territory around Caesarea, especially those on the northern Plain of Sharon. We want to consolidate the farms and lease them to commercial olive growers."

"I remember your father as Amram ben Eleazar's partner and friend. I would see him at the Great Synagogue with you and your aunt when you were little."

I smiled, remembering that he wouldn't have seen Binyamin with us. Binyamin could never sit still long enough for the reading of the Torah.

"Oh, yes," I said, nodding, but I really didn't remember him from the Synagogue, only from his visits to Amram's house to participate in the daily recitation of *Kaddish* in memory of Noah. But then I did recall Noah's telling me he'd invested some of our fathers' capital to expand Gershon's import business beyond Alexandria to the upcountry Jews in the villages and towns along the Nile. Gershon believed they too would appreciate a full-bodied deep purple wine from the Holy Land, and Noah knew they'd pay the price for a wine that hadn't been filtered on Shabbat.

"In those days, Amram and I would sponsor the visits of sages from Jerusalem to give lectures at the Great Synagogue, and we'd host families who wanted to settle in Alexandria."

After three spaced taps on the door frame, Gershon's Nubian houseboy, Khukare, padded in with a gold-leaf tray of miniature pita loaves arranged on a bed of greens and stuffed with chopped apricots and almonds. He eased the tray onto a carved acacia side table, unfurled two starched Indian cotton napkins, and handed each of us a silver cup of cooled water scented with rose petals. When Gershon thanked him, Khukare bowed low, his tall ebony frame folding at the waist, his long black braids brushing the floor as his forehead met his knees. Then the *whoosh* of his tunic melted in the air as he turned and left.

Gershon continued to reminisce about Amram, how they'd meet at the Great Gymnasium to throw the javelin or discus, sometimes with my father joining them. Then, if it was before Shabbat, they'd relieve themselves of the week's weariness in the incense-scented Roman-style baths. Beginning with the *frigidarium*, they'd progress to the *tepidarium* and then to the steamy *caldarium* before returning to the *tepidarium* to be wrapped in carbasus linen and have their bodies massaged with spicy unguents. But I was more interested in what he had to say later about his business in Caesarea. Maybe I'd learn enough to embellish my own story about being there.

"Judea is not a great exporter of wine, but the grapes produce a wine that Alexandrian and upcountry Jews are willing to pay dearly for. I buy from the vineyards on the northern Plain of Sharon, where the grapes grow as if they were wild. You'll see this land is quite expensive—I hope not too expensive for you and your father—and then during the dry season, I bring the wine south to Caesarea along the Shephalah Road. At that time, when the caravans are running and all the merchants are converging on Caesarea, I also buy cassia bark from India for those who like to add cinnamon to their wine. Then I use a Roman shipping company to transport my cargo to Egypt."

We paused to sip the scented water from our cups.

"I don't understand. Why do you sometimes use Samson's company but other times a Roman company to ship your wine?"

"I use the Greeks, Phoenicians, and Romans to ship my ordinary wines. They are far better sailors than the Jews, who have always feared the sea. But I use only Samson's ships to transport my most precious cargo, the one I stake my reputation on. As we speak, the *Orion* is carrying the most renowned wine in the Empire to the one customer in Caesarea who can afford it, the procurator himself, Tiberius Julius Alexander. This wine, Faustian Falernian, comes from the central slopes of Mount

Falernus, the finest wine-producing region in all of Italy. After a series of frosts, its Aglianico grapes are harvested, and then, after the juice is fermented, the wine is stored and aged in clay amphorae for at least a decade. I trust only Samson to transport this wine. Other shippers would be only too eager to steal my cargo and substitute a cheaper wine with a counterfeit label."

Having concluded whatever he intended to say about his business, he turned to the tray and handed me a stuffed pita. It filled my mouth with a gritty tang that flowered into a spicy sweetness. When he'd taken his time to enjoy several, he plucked a dandelion leaf from the tray, savored its bitterness, and then wiped a few crumbs from his hands and mouth with his napkin. I did the same.

An easy silence followed until his conversation drifted back to Amram.

"Amram. So many tragedies for one man to endure. I remember when his wife and daughters were killed during the pogrom."

That terrible night, already ten years ago but its memory still so fresh in my mind. Amram and Noah were attending a meeting to organize an appeal to Caligula. Leah and the girls were home when a gang of thugs trapped them in their house, set their furnishings ablaze, and then mocked their cries as the smoke suffocated them and the hissing flames devoured them. During the mourning period that followed, one that stretched well into the next year, an indivisible bond formed between Noah and me, two motherless souls drawn together for a tenderness our fathers were too distraught to provide.

"Yes," I said with a shiver, "those were horrific days for our people."

This time the silence that gathered around us smelled like darkness.

"I'm afraid the days ahead may be even worse." His gaze thickened, and his brow furrowed before he spoke again.

"All might seem quiet in Judea, especially to a stranger, but an underground resistance is bubbling throughout the land. Since the death of Herod Agrippa, there's been a resurgence of

Jewish nationalism and with it, a wave of civil disorder that Cuspius Fadus and now Alexander have been unable to suppress. In the cause of a Judea ruled once again by Judeans, Jewish peasants are attacking Roman soldiers and anyone else, Jew or Gentile, they suspect is collaborating with Rome. Shepherds are dropping their crooks; farmers, their hoes; and smithies, their hammers to take up the sword with escaped slaves, thieves, and anyone else who has nothing more to lose. In addition, false prophets and pseudo-messiahs have emerged, promising to deliver Judea spiritually from the yoke of Roman oppression. Their growing number of followers likewise threatens Rome.

"I'm sure our sages spoke at the Great Synagogue about Theudas, the Judean rebel who promised to split the waters of the Jordan as Moses divided the Red Sea. Suspecting that Theudas intended to use the event to incite an anti-Roman uprising, Fadus sent a cavalry unit to the Jordan Valley to drown the peasants in their own blood. His horsemen in their red cloaks and enameled cuirasses not only slew hundreds of Theudas's disciples, all unarmed by the way, but they took the rest as prisoners. Capturing Theudas himself, they beheaded him and carried his head to Jerusalem."

Suddenly a fishy mixture of apricots and almonds surged up my gorge and coated the back of my throat with bile. My stomach had grasped what my mind still struggled to acknowledge, that if our secret leaks out beyond the Seed of Abraham—and maybe it already has—the Romans would slaughter every alchemist in the Empire. They'd gladly make an example of any Jew who appeared to be a threat, political or economic, real or imagined. And along with us, they'd crucify as collaborators our kin, companions, and servants to make a statement more savage and far-reaching than any pogrom. But that wasn't all. The *Sicarii* could regard Eran, Judah, and me as traitors, as business people supportive of the Roman status quo, and slaughter us in our beds.

With my bowels turning to water, I feigned a headache, levered myself out of the chaise, and excused myself with haste.

Chapter 6

Morning of the Fifth Day

I BROODED IN my cabin for the rest of the voyage, even while the failing winds detained us somewhere west of Gaza. Unable to eat, read, sleep, or exchange ordinary remarks, too spent from the dread that tightened around my throat like a garrote, I lay in a blurry insomnia wishing only for *Soteria*, the Greek goddess of safety, preservation, and deliverance, to guide Eran, Judah, and me to a place neither the Romans nor the Zealots could ever find. I tried to imagine my reunion with Judah, but even that sweet fantasy couldn't rescue me from the stranglehold of dread.

Phoebe fluttered about my bedside. When she wasn't massaging my temples with a lavender-scented oil, she was fanning away the breathless heat, going only to Eli's galley to either brew a pot of cannabis tea to stimulate my appetite or tempt me with something from his hearth. Nothing worked. By the evening of the second day in my cabin, I told her I must be seasick, that we Jews were indeed poor sailors. But the fib was all too obvious. The sea was a sheet of polished metal, without a breath of wind to pit its mirrored surface or whip our sails or rock the hull or temper the sun.

My doldrums were relieved only by the fifth morning when I heard above the wash of the sea the mournful screech of a lone gull spiraling overhead. A moment later, emerging through the portside doors onto the afterdeck, I saw a squadron of them wheeling above the deckhouse, dipping low, some settling fore, some aft, others flitting here and there, one already with a strip of blood-streaked meat hanging from its bill. Land at last! The long, slow curve of the shoreline was sliding toward us. Soon I'd see the *Sebastos*, the famous harbor Herod the Great built and named for his emperor, and be greeted at its gateway by six colossal statues, three starboard, three port, each portraying a member of Augustus's family atop a column that would tower over the tallest mast.

I remembered Hector, Phoebe's and my tutor, telling us about the harbor's construction: That Augustus sent his engineers to assist Herod's architects. That thousands of slaves and conscripts worked furiously to complete the project in a mere twelve years. That the breakwaters as well as the harbor's submarine foundation, jetties, and walls are made of Roman concrete. And that the aggregate stone of this concrete is held together by a special mortar made from a volcanic ash imported from central Italy so that it hardens in contact with water.

Scores of grain ships, their sails stripped to enter the harbor, queued up ahead of us. As her captain performed a post-sail sacrifice on the poop deck in gratitude for a safe arrival, each ship wafted the odor of burning flesh and smudged the sky with curls of smoke. At the same time, harbor tugs lined up in the choppy sea outside the northern breakwater so each team of husky, sun-glazed rowers could grab the next ship's tow rope. Trailing along until she approached the mouth of the harbor, each ship in turn dropped her long starboard oar to turn south and then southeast toward the quays.

Once inside the harbor, each ship passed between the windowed stone cube that was the harbormaster's house and a forty-meter high, three-tiered lighthouse. This loftiest of towers, similar in design to our Pharos Lighthouse but less than a third of its height, was named Drusion for Augustus's stepson and likely successor, Nero Claudius Drusus Germanicus. We followed another but more luxurious merchantman with a latrine suspended over the open water beyond the sternpost. She slid toward the southern breakwater and the unbroken line of *horrea*, the vaulted warehouses lining the wide promenade along the lip of the harbor. Splitting the current, her wake followed her like a ruffled-edged cape until she was moored to a huge stone ring on the quay.

As the *Orion* slid through the gateway and turned southeast, a cool, fishy tang poured into my lungs. Directly ahead of us, backlit by the morning sun, facing northwest toward Rome rather than southeast toward Jerusalem, the Temple of Augustus and Roma commanded the cityscape from a lofty platform atop the harbor's land quay. Just as I'd begun to admire its symmetry, a tangle of ropes flew about me, shifting my gaze downward to the promenade where I saw a kaleidoscope of colors and patterns resolve themselves into a crowd of onlookers. I can't say in what order, but after that, I heard the blare of a trumpet from one of the watchtowers, the shriek of a whistle on board, the groan of ropes growing taut, the whine of hatches opening and closing, and the thunder of hundreds of passengers tramping toward the gangplank while bare-chested stevedores swarmed the wharf to unload the cargo.

I wanted to linger on deck, to scan the expanse of faces for the one I longed to see, to have the secret pleasure of watching him for even the briefest moment, but there was little time. Phoebe was waiting with our bags, and I owed a thank you to Eli and a good-bye to Gershon. So I stepped away from the gunwale and set out to find them.

Part Four: Caesarea Maritima

Chapter 7

First Day in Caesarea, Thursday Afternoon

GERSHON VOLUNTEERED to shepherd us along the promenade until Judah claimed us. Pressed into a single file, we inched our way around clots of sun-drenched pedestrians in brilliantly colored garments, some strongly perfumed, most babbling in Greek, the men lavishly bearded, the women's necks draped with silver and gold. Ragged beggars followed us. Many were idlers, but some were crippled, blind, or sick with dropsy, exanthema, elephantiasis, or, most hideous of all, mosaic leprosy. Inhaling flames of the midday heat, the pavement burning through the soles of my sandals, I kept swiveling my head to scan the crowd for that one face wreathed in black curls. Oppressed by the bustle, the stink of lumbering drays, and the shouts of vendors hawking skewers of grilled lamb coated with flies, I asked that we take a few minutes to rest and give Judah a chance to spot us instead.

With Gershon and his entourage, we must have been quite the spectacle, judging by the idlers. A few simply gawked, but most pelted us with hostile stares, some with their nostrils flared, others with their jaws clenched, lips compressed, teeth bared, or fists balled. I could feel their hatred buzzing through me. In addition to Khukare, who carried his master's personal effects in a pair of Numidian leather bags slung over each shoulder and across his chest, two other Nubian servants accompanied Gershon.

Like Khukare, they were resplendent in their white linen tunics and silver-buckled *calcei*, but their bodies were broader than his. A pair of reigning giants with forearms like battering rams, they each supported against their cyclopean neck an

33

enormous wicker trunk trimmed in leather and brass. The face of one, however, was disfigured by a ropelike scar that puckered his left cheek and pulled at the corner of his mouth, which suggested to me that he, if not both, functioned as Gershon's bodyguard as well as his porter. Gershon himself was draped in an elegant, almost effeminate robe of scarlet silk fashioned in the Greek style.

At last I heard a single set of footfalls spring out of the harbor's hum and clatter. I gripped Phoebe's hand and turned to hear, "Welcome to Caesarea. I've been looking all over for you." Rather than his usual *colobium*, a coarse, short-sleeved gray workingman's tunic, Judah wore a sleeveless green tunic of Indian cotton with a thin leather belt at his waist. I wanted to believe he'd dressed up for me, but he gave no sign that he'd missed me in the ten months since he'd left Alexandria. Rather, his eyes slid over me to nod to the others in a generic greeting. But perhaps I'd been expecting too much. While I'd been fanned by a breeze on the afterdeck, he'd been baking under a pitiless sun.

After an introduction, which Judah and Gershon sealed with a handshake, Judah took our bags. Then he and Gershon guided us to the nearest street, which runs east-west one block south of the main east-west thoroughfare, the *Decumanus Maximus*. According to Judah, the streets in Caesarea, like other cities designed in the Greek tradition, are laid out in an orthogonal grid that delimits blocks of equal size. As we walked east along the *decumanus* that runs tangent to the southeast corner of the Temple—the Romans refer to all their east-west streets as *decumani*—Phoebe and I looked southward through fleeting gaps in the crowd to glimpse pieces of the stadium, and beyond that, of the palace, theater, and city wall, but we got a close-up view of the side of the Temple, its formal gardens, Corinthian colonnades, and platform of well-carved ashlars.

After two blocks of neatly arranged white stone houses guarded by serried ranks of dwarf plane trees, we turned north onto the *Cardo Maximus*, the main north-south thoroughfare— the Romans refer to their north-south streets as *cardines*—and the block where Gershon's host, Lucius Didius Bassus, lives. As soon as we approached the walls of his estate, a hound-faced doorkeeper swung open the vine-covered iron gate. Beyond it, I marveled at a perfectly proportioned marble mansion enclosed by a hedge of fragrant rosemary and fronted by a garden furnished with teak benches flanked by cages of trilling songbirds. In the center of the garden, a stone fountain sprayed its iridescent shower into a pool of water lilies while statues peered from behind mulberry trees, and date palms tossed their arching shadows onto an alabaster walkway edged with yellow poppies. Once we exchanged the usual compliments and assurances with Gershon, we waved our good-byes and continued on our way.

WE CROSSED ONTO the shadier west side of the *Cardo Maximus* and resumed walking toward The Three Graces, the inn just inside the Northern Gate where Judah said he'd reserved a private room for us. While rambling on about the weather and the cost of beans, he pointed out the local landmarks, the first being the next cross street, the *Decumanus Maximus*. Eran's shop, he said, would be a half a block to our left, and his house would be a block and a half to our right.

Clearly, Judah was proud that Eran had prime locations for both his house and business, but my heart sank. The Northern Gate could hardly have been farther from Eran's house. I tried to comfort myself with the thought that there might be few if any other inns in the city expressly for unescorted women and that The Three Graces might in fact be the closest if not the nicest. Or else I hoped that he deliberately chose an inn at a distance to be discreet about our relationship. But to no avail. My spirits spiraled downward toward those darkest of all places, hopelessness and mortification. Had it not been for Eran's recipe—its secrets could be circulating at this very moment—I'd have doubted the sense of the entire trip.

Our merged shadows pulled us along the mica-flecked pavement as we glanced at shops, monuments, arcades, mansions, and tenements. Freedmen and slaves, their ears punched with holes, overtook us on the walkway while litters, sedan chairs, and caravans rocked past us on the thoroughfare. Judah pointed out other attractions along the way, the best *kapēleion* for pastries and the best apothecary shop for herbs as if I'd come all the way to Caesarea to eat pastry and ease a headache.

I noticed the inns, of course. They identify themselves with a gaily decorated façade, a notice boasting their fare, and a colorful flag. The flag for The Hercules was the most flamboyant. It depicted its namesake, massive and muscular, holding the golden apples of the Hesperides behind his back as he wearily leaned on his club. The flag for another, The Doe, left nothing to the imagination in its display of women cavorting in forbidden ways with men and other women. By then, we found ourselves in a lackluster neighborhood of scrawny children; narrow, foul-smelling alleyways; and dilapidated dwellings, no doubt the homes of poor artisans and starving freedmen.

Riding an elusive breeze were the stench of human feces and the tang of an astringent, the combination adding to the ever-present reek of dung drying in the gutters. Across the street, squads of men with earlocks, Hebraic beards, and long striped tunics were scrubbing excrement off the stucco exterior of their humble little synagogue, sweeping up rubble from its cracked flagstone walkway, and assessing the damage to its entryway, the double doors canting against their shattered jambs. Deep blue tassels swayed at the corners of their mantles while outrage pinched at the corners of their mouths. Other men awaited their turn with fresh rags, buckets of water, and pots of ash while baring their teeth and waggling their heads. Others cast up their eyes, some with tears drilling down their cheeks. Their bodies rocked forward and back as they murmured their prayers, whether for liberation or revenge I could not tell.

"What on earth happened here?" I asked Judah while my eyes smarted from the caustic ash.

"Eran spoke of this latest desecration at breakfast. Not that he'd have seen news of it posted in the Forum among notices for the next public execution or the penalty for emptying out a chamber pot in the street after sunrise. Instead, he seems to have his own grapevine."

The satisfaction in Judah's voice told me he was pleased his brother was involved in Caesarea's Jewish community.

But then his forehead creased like a rumpled sheet. "The favorite sport here for off-duty soldiers is goading Jews. But don't misunderstand me. The Jews don't need to be goaded. Their community is already smoldering with rage. Jews are exempt from military service—what they call the blood tax—so their monetary taxes to Rome are draconian. And don't forget, they also pay a tithe to support the priesthood and Temple in Jerusalem. But more than the civil taxes, they resent being ruled by impious pagans who strip them of their dignity and despoil their shrines. So the mere sight of a Roman is provocation enough. Claudius's mistake was allowing local recruits with their entrenched loyalties and animosities to serve in the garrison here. Some of them must have picked this spot for last night's carousing. The neighbors heard drunken howls and whoops of savage laughter, the thud of bricks against wood, and the screech of metal against stone till well past the fading of the morning star."

"Oh, Judah. What will these poor people do?"

"There will be reprisals, Miriam. Of that I can assure you."

I was taken aback by the fierceness in his voice.

ONE MORE BLOCK of huddled tenements, and I spotted the flag for The Three Graces unfurling in a passing breeze. Three lithe maidens, the goddesses of Joy, Cheer, and Beauty, festooned with diaphanous streamers, danced in a loving embrace. The inn itself had a porticoed marble façade guarded by griffins gazing past a copper fountain into a garden-edged oval pool. But upon close inspection, I could see that the marble was faux, the portico crumbling, the griffins cracked, the garden overgrown, the fountain dry, and the pool a waterless basin of chipped tiles and nesting vermin. Then, just beyond the inn, a stable yard sat soaking up the sun. While its chariots, carts, and coaches painted their boxy shadows on the cylindrical towers of the North Gate, fountains of its gritty dust clouded the sky, and the stink of its tethered animals fouled the air.

An ancient, milky-eyed doorkeeper in threadbare livery and an ill-fitting hat sat on an inverted tub inside the shade of the portico. He welcomed us in a surprisingly elegant voice and called for the *puer* to take our bags. Then the *hospita*, a sturdy, big-breasted woman, her cheeks stained with red ochre and her eyes lined with kohl, ushered us into the public dining room. Once grand, it had vivid murals of the harbor, a mosaic floor depicting the Twelve Olympians, and couch cushions of embroidered Indian cotton albeit worn. Its linen-covered tables were laden with cut glass vases, bronze trays, brass candelabra, and silver craters.

When an unbidden waiter brought us silver goblets of pomegranate wine, I saw in the mirror of mine a glossy face streaked with dust and a crown of braids askew and uncoiling. My poor Phoebe didn't look much better with her hair matted, her face flushed, and her coarse gray tunic stamped with wrinkles. But Judah looked fresh. The only evidence of a barbarous sun was that his black curls had lost some of their bounce, hugging his head more like a helmet than a wreath.

After a few halfhearted sips, Phoebe excused herself to unpack our bags, leaving Judah and me to face each other across a massive mahogany table. Following a stilted exchange, he explained in an unnaturally rapid stream how he found Eran.

"I knew he ran off to Judea and began an apprenticeship with a jeweler. But no one heard a word after that. So I figured he probably settled in a city, unless he was working as an itinerant jeweler, in which case he could be anywhere, and I'd have to look for him in Jerusalem during the Passover. So I started right here in Caesarea. What other Judean city would be as cosmopolitan as Alexandria and have a Greek-speaking population? When I went to a goldsmith's shop to ask about a jeweler named Eran, I didn't even have to mention his port-wine stain, which he keeps covered anyway with a wig that drops curls over his forehead. They knew right away I was asking about the man who calls himself Eran ben Zahav, a member of their guild with a shop fronting the Forum. I rushed over, and as soon as I introduced myself, he invited me to stay as his houseguest."

Judah gave me a pointed look while silence filled the room. "Miriam, now tell me why you've come."

That's Judah, I thought, as direct as ever. Rummaging through my mental closet while picking at the threads of my tunic, not knowing where to begin or how much to tell, I took a deep breath and spaced out each word to keep my voice steady.

"When I read your letter, I became concerned that Eran had a recipe like yours for perfecting copper. I want to find out how he got it."

All at once his lips parted, his lids retracted, and his eyebrows lifted as if he were a marionette manipulated by a single string. Then in a gust of exasperation, he raked his hands through his hair, parked his elbows on the table, and leaned forward.

"Miriam, listen to me."

I cradled my upper arms.

"My goal at the moment is to get to know my brother and help him manage his business. He's a master jeweler specializing in presentation pieces for important clients including Alexander himself. So any recipe is peripheral to my life right now. I wrote the letter to you as a courtesy, to assure you I was safe, and my mission to find Eran was successful. I mentioned the recipe as an interesting aside, a fluke. Yes, it irks me, but I never expected you to attach such importance to it. Besides, we already have our own recipe for perfecting copper. We don't need Eran's."

He didn't have to add that the responsibility for two unescorted women was a burden. The tightness of his shoulders told me that.

At that moment, my spirits were in freefall, but I knew one thing Judah didn't—that Eran's recipe was of the utmost importance if we valued our Holy Secrets, our lives, and the safety of those we love. What I didn't know was how I was going to trace its source without Judah's cooperation.

Chapter 8

Second Day, Late Friday Afternoon

"NO, MIRIAM, THAT'S wrong, all wrong."

Phoebe was pointing to my tunic, compressing her lips, and shaking her head. We were in our room, the most private chamber in the inn, a Spartan, low-raftered, saggy-floored attic *cella* overlooking the street. The watery eastern sunlight and a smoking oil lamp hanging from a joist struggled against the shadows along with two lit candelabra, each on a tripod stand, each spilling a puddle of weak yellow light onto the adjacent lumpy cot. I'd been trying on a crimson, short-sleeved, ankle-length tunic over a white, floor-length *tunica interior* with a Roman-style gold *instita* embroidered along its hem.

"Forget the crimson. Too much color. You're not going to the theater, Miriam. You're going to someone's home. Put on the blue one." Posed like an artist with her head cocked to the left, she directed me as she sat on the wooden crate at the foot of her cot.

Phoebe could be rather officious at times like this when she fixed on the importance of an occasion. Tonight Judah would escort me to Shabbat dinner at Eran's house, my first opportunity to meet him and make a good impression. I could see she'd decided on the blue before I'd even tried on the crimson. She'd taken it out of the rattan chest near my cot and laid it out across the rickety table under the window. What's more, she'd folded back the shutters on their rusty hinges so its sheen could catch the thin shafts of daylight. Unfortunately, she'd also ushered in the heat from the street and the stink from the stable yard. The room smelled like an old dog. But at such times, I was at her mercy and knew better than to argue.

We'd gone in the morning to a *balnea*, a small, privately owned bathhouse on the *cardo* one block east of ours. As with many *balneae* these days, women are allowed to use them from daybreak to noon, men, from early afternoon to sundown. Phoebe had marched in like an overseer. She tested the temperature of the baths and inspected the fingernails of the attendants. She made sure the olive oil was warm, the towels fluffy, and the sheets clean. In the *tepidarium*, she fingered the edge of the *strigilis* before she let the slave use it to scrape away the dirt, oil, and dead skin from my body, and later, when we were back in the *tepidarium* for my massage, she sniffed the unguents to check their freshness and ensure the scent I chose was appropriate.

But she insisted on doing the rest of the grooming rituals herself. Once we got back to the inn, we crouched on the warped floorboards under the cobwebs festooning the *cella*'s eaves while she bathed my hands and face in the washbasin the *puer* fills each morning. Then she cut my nails and rubbed my face with a pumice stone to remove the stray hairs above my upper lip and around my eyebrows. She gathered my curls in a loose bun at the nape of my neck, which she held in place with long gold pins and dressed with a gold-threaded net. Finally, I watched in a polished bronze hand mirror as she set ringlets around my face with a *calamistrum*. Holding it by its handle, she heated it in the candle flame and then wound wisps of my hair around it.

All the while she asked me about Judah: Did I still love him? Did I want to marry him?

"Phoebe, you know I didn't want to marry Noah. And you know I don't want to be a mother, not only because I don't want to die like mine did, but because I want to do something different with my life, to study alchemy and find a way to heal both the human spirit and the spirit of base metals. But I was attracted to Judah because of his work, his values—especially the simplicity that frames his life and his art—and because he awakened in me that longing to know him as a woman knows a man."

"So, during your mourning period for Noah, did you ever think of marrying him once that year was over?"

"I suppose Judah's the only man I ever thought of marrying,

if I considered getting married at all. But don't forget, Phoebe, he's already twenty-seven, well past the marriage age, and besides, he's never asked me. He's treated me like a good friend and trusted colleague, but only once, in an unguarded moment when we were alone in his shop, and I tripped into his arms, did he show any desire for me. That was two years ago. Entwined for that briefest moment, I felt the hammering of his heart and the rise of his manhood. But he pulled away immediately and told me he could never give me the life I was meant for. He said that if we indulged our passion, I'd have to bear the stigma on my wedding night or worse yet, endure with my child, as his mother had with him, the invectives of an unforgiving community."

"Miriam, of course he wouldn't declare his love for you while you were betrothed to Noah or, for that matter later, while you were still mourning his death."

I could see in the mirror that to match her flinty tone, her eyes flared with an ill-disguised impatience. So I just glued mine to the floor while she fastened the sleeves of the favored tunic with gold clasps.

"But things are different now." Her tone had honeyed to a lilt. "You're both free to marry; he has a father's name now, and with his inheritance from Saul, he was able to satisfy the mortgage your father held on his shop."

After adjusting the tunic over the *tunica interior*, she girded me with a *strophium* to gather the fabric under my breasts and arrange the skirt in soft folds above the *instita*. Finally, she dressed my ears with gold hoops, clad my feet in leather sandals tied with blue silk ribbons, and draped me in a light woolen himation, which she pinned at my shoulder with a gold brooch.

"If you hadn't given it to Binyamin, we could have used your mother's fibula to bring you luck tonight instead of this plain brooch."

"Now, Phoebe, that was the least I could do when he left for Capua."

But I don't think she heard me. She was doing her final proprietary inspection.

"There," she said with a self-congratulatory nod. "Now, you're ready to track down that alchemical recipe and charm your man in the process."

I wish it had been that simple.

Chapter 9

Friday (Shabbat) Evening

THE NORTHERN section of the city, where most of the Jews live, was wrapped in the stillness of Shabbat as Judah and I walked along the hushed *Cardo Maximus* toward Eran's house. The bathhouses had emptied, the laborers had trudged home, the stall owners had packed up their wares, and the shopkeepers had closed their shutters. As dusk eased into darkness, I was buoyed up by the savory aromas of Shabbat—especially the freshly baked bread—and the hope of finding the scroll with Eran's recipe.

"Miriam, I hope you're not going to quiz Eran tonight about the provenance of his recipe."

"Well, if he won't tell you, I can hardly expect him to tell me, can I? Besides, I'd like to think I'm shrewder than that." *Does he think I'm a dolt? Still, I shouldn't have alerted him with that last jab. Who knows what scheme I might have to engineer and whether he might try to foil it in a misguided sense of loyalty to Eran? But I'm certainly not about to give up, as he apparently has, just because Eran refused to tell how he got it.*

We passed the little synagogue, its exterior immaculate, its walkway cleared and set with new flagstone. I heard the chant of worshippers through the newly hung, half-open doors and caught a glimpse inside of the eternal flame dancing above the Ark. All the while, despite my strides, Judah managed to keep a pace or two ahead, an occasional backward glance his only assurance I still followed and my only assurance he remembered I was there.

"Well, tell me more about Eran. What's he like?" I shouted the question to the back of his head to make him wait up.

I knew only that seventeen years ago, Eran had disowned his father, stormed out of their house, and run off to Judea. His mother, Saul's late wife Dinah, sick with mania for more than twenty years, died a few years ago. She had only the one child. Like her, Judah's mother, a silversmith named Ruth, died fifteen years ago without having any other children. So with Saul's death, Eran came to be Judah's only living relative.

He stopped in the middle of the pavement, turned his head, and momentarily closed his eyes, as if to shore up his patience while I trotted up to him. "He's not like other people, Miriam. He's had a hard life beginning with a sick mother and an inattentive father who lied to him repeatedly. Who knows how long and hard he had to work before he could establish himself? And then he has this port-wine stain that stigmatizes him as impure according to Jewish Law. So it's no wonder he has a volatile temper.

"But in his calm moments, he's a gifted goldsmith, a shrewd businessman, and a patriot. He raises money for the peasants who, to pay their taxes, had to sell off their land to commercial farmers. Anyway, you'll see what he's like, but give him time. He dislikes most people when he first meets them. So he's not easy to get to know."

"It sounds like you're not so sure yourself about your relationship with—"

"Oh, no. I'm sure." His tone was as resolute as the flash in his eyes. "He's my brother, and I'm here to make him my friend."

Rounding the corner onto the *Decumanus Maximus,* I saw the upper stories of limestone mansions peeking above leafy groves of flowering hibiscus. As I passed each estate, I'd part the foliage and gape at the colonnades and arcades, balconies and porticoes, loggias and statuary, arbors and fishponds, waterfalls and fountains. And then, near the end of the second block, Judah turned, and I followed him through a portal into a miniature park of smooth lawns and fanciful topiary screened by a grove of Mediterranean cypress.

He took my arm to guide me along a sinuous walkway fringed with peonies. Mounted alongside on tall iron stands, scented torches cut through the darkness and threw their sparks to the sky.

"Just remember," he whispered as we approached the richly carved front doors of the mansion, "he's earned all of this himself, every bit of it."

When had Judah begun to value ostentation?

A lanky, stringy-necked freedman, his skin pockmarked by acne, some pustules still in bloom, met us at the entryway. Escorting us into the atrium, he took our wraps and seated us on a dark mahogany bench guarded by urns of red roses and illuminated by lamps floating in the *impluvium*, the shallow sunken pool in the center of the atrium. His mouth was so stuffed with crooked teeth that I wondered how he could speak. When he did, his voice was slippery but with a distinct nasal quality. "Good Shabbat to you, Mr. Judah. Is this the beautiful guest from Alexandria you promised us?" Then, facing me, he displayed his upper teeth and the gum line above them and bowed. "Welcome and Good Shabbat to you, Miss bat Isaac. I'm Jabin, Mr. Eran's assistant. Thank you for gracing our home tonight."

Two olive-skinned houseboys—they could have been twins the way their eyes filled their faces—brought us a small cedar serving table bearing towels and two stone pots, which they filled with perfumed water from a silver vessel so we could wash our hands and feet. As soon as we finished, they served us each a goblet of Palestinian wine and then withdrew.

Jabin returned sometime later to usher us past a pair of terracotta Etruscan *hydriae*, brick and cream-colored ornamental water jugs, about forty inches high, each with a lid bearing a life-size head of Apollo. Hector once told me jars this large were used to store grain. Had he seen these, he'd surely have said they came from a palace. The two priceless vessels flanked a set of carved ebony doors, probably to Eran's study. A moment later, we crossed the atrium's polished marble floor, skirted around the *impluvium*, and found ourselves inside Eran's cavernous *triclinium*.

My eyes were so overwhelmed by the excess that at first I saw only an abstract field of color and light. But the speckles gradually coalesced into a vaulted ceiling of frescoed panels, plaster walls covered with vivid tapestries, and clouds of dark blue irises brooding in their Athenian vases. The sofas, armchairs, and benches as well as the dining couches were padded with cushions of Chinese silk and illuminated by an eclectic mix of ornate candelabra, some bronze, others brass and silver, one more flamboyant than the next, each resting on a marble lamp stand as thick as a tree trunk.

Given the clutter, it was impossible to catalogue the rest of the furnishings. The cabinets, some of citron wood, others of rosewood, acacia, mahogany, and teak, were laden with garish presentation pieces: goblets and craters, trays and candelabra, platters and bowls, ladles and carving knives. Likewise the tops of the chests were strewn with statues and busts, vases and jeweled hand mirrors, figurines and marble plaques, censers and primitive masks, and cut glass lamps that spread the cloying scent of rancid olive oil throughout the room. But as I scanned the perimeter, my eyes stumbled on an island in the far corner of rigidly arranged, bulky oak furniture and lit upon a man sitting forward on a cushioned armchair, staring like a viper into this sea of excess.

Having expected Eran to resemble Judah, I couldn't have been more surprised when, in a waft of expensive fragrance, he emerged from the shadows. An emerald green *synthesis*, a loose gown Romans wear at their own dinner parties, this one studded with multicolored Alexandrine glass beads, almost masked the paunch on his otherwise solid frame, and he wore enough rings to smother the fingers of both hands. To confirm that he was indeed Eran, I looked to his forehead for that indelible stain, but the curls dangling from the crown of his wig blanketed his brow.

"So you're the Miriam Judah's been telling me about. What brings you to Caesarea?"

"My father and I want to buy up and consolidate some of the small farms outside the city so we can lease them to commercial olive growers."

"So you're not here just to keep an eye on Judah?" A phony heartiness attended his forced laughter, but his eyes stayed hard like little black pebbles. "My dear young lady, if you buy up those farms, you'll be displacing those Jews who are being forced to sell their land to pay the emperor's rapacious taxes. Instead of being self-sufficient as they've been for generations, they'll end up working for a pittance either as laborers in the city or as indentured servants for you and your father."

I'd touched a nerve. His face darkened, and with a convulsive jerk of his head, his wig shifted, exposing a sliver of his birthmark.

Jabin interrupted to save us from an expanding silence and conduct us to a set of four dining couches around a low, square bronze-legged table topped with onyx. As soon as we took our places—Eran moved swiftly despite his bulk—the look-alike houseboys set before us napkins and crystal goblets, which they filled from a freshly mixed crater of wine and honey-sweetened water, and then offered the first course, a platter of steaming vegetables in a pungent mustard sauce. While we sipped the wine, they paraded in with covered platters of grilled fish, roasted fowl, and stewed lamb as well as an array of condiments, salads, and dips, all of which they set on a nearby sideboard and then fluttered about ready to serve us.

"The Romans are draining our economy and dividing our people. That's why so many of our peasants have to sell." Eran picked up the napkin to dab the saliva that foamed at the corners of his mouth. "But it's not just the taxes, as horrendous as they are. A peasant has to pay a third of his produce, a quarter of his fruit, and half of his oil and wine. And don't let me forget the salt tax and the dues to maintain the roads and bridges, but at least with Herod the money stayed here. Now the money that doesn't enrich the procurators' coffers goes directly to Rome. Our only hope rests with the *Sicarii*."

"With the *Sicarii*? Aren't they terrorists?" My voice broke like an adolescent boy's. "They target other Jews—"

Eran stretched out a ring-laden hand to correct me. "They're not terrorists, my dear. They're freedom fighters." He spoke calmly, his voice as smooth as custard, but the edge of his birthmark had turned from pink to violet.

"Miriam, the politics here are complicated." Judah's voice was steady, but his eyes rebuked me.

And I felt a naughty delight in his discomfort.

Nobody touched the food.

"Can I refill your goblet or serve you from one of the platters?" Jabin's voice was more slippery than ever as he rose to a stoop, ready to chase the silence.

"The *Sicarii* target those Jews who are traitors to our people, those who not only profit from the misery of other Jews but point their fingers at our patriots so the Romans can round them up and crucify them." Although he continued to speak in a controlled voice, his face had hardened, and blotches of sweat began to darken his *synthesis*.

At the time, I simply thought he'd drunk too much wine.

"Surely the *Sicarii* only exacerbate the very conditions that make the peasants' plight so wretched here." I sounded like Eli's parrot.

With the cry of a madman, Eran sprang to his feet, stretched his neck like a cobra ready to strike, and thrust his contorted face into mine. His eyes fixed and challenging, his teeth clenched, his nostrils flared, his lips thinned, his breath sour, his wig askew, his birthmark fully exposed, deep purple and luminous, he spewed his rage in a stream of venom.

"You simpering ignoramus! You impertinent fool. How dare you contradict me!"

Where was Judah now?

I was dumbfounded. After all, Eran himself reeked of Roman wealth and manners. But I certainly wasn't going to argue the point. It was Shabbat, I was a guest, and I was here not to make an enemy but to find a recipe and determine its provenance. So, in a pretense of smoothing my hair, I covered my ear with my flattened palm. Then thumbing open the catch at the back of my earring, gripping the hoop between my first two fingers, concealing the rest of it as I pulled it free, I lowered my hand and slipped the earring inside my *strophium*.

"Good heavens," I exclaimed. "I've lost my earring! That must have been the tinkle I heard in the atrium. Excuse me, but

I must get it. The pair belonged to my mother." So, feigning alarm, I got up from the couch, steadying myself against its edge so no one could see my legs trembling, and headed back to those oily, dark doors.

Chapter 10

Late Friday (Shabbat) Evening

PLUCKING AT MY skirts to raise the hem, I slid my sandals along the marble floor so no one could hear that I was heading directly to the ebony doors. Breathless with the hope of finding the scroll but tasting uncertainty in the slime on my tongue, I reached for the silver door handles, eager to feel their dry coolness in my sweaty hands and hear the latch spring back.

But no. The handles resisted. First one. Then the other. Then both. Nothing. I tried pushing them, pulling them, jiggling them. Again nothing. The doors were locked.

Tight.

Now what?

For all his rings—the cameos; the one set with a round, blue glass cabochon; his garnet seal ring; others bejeweled with pearls, chalcedony, and amethyst—he wasn't wearing any with a key attached. Most men wear ring keys since their clothes have no pockets. *So where does he keep the ring key for his study?* My eyes scanned the atrium for a hiding place: the bench, the dimly lit *impluvium*, and the urns. Fleshy blooms all over. In every urn and vase. Except the *hydriae*.

I lifted the lid and thrust my arm inside one of them. My hand stirred something dry, scaly, reptilian. Yikes! I sprang back as if I'd touched Vulcan's forge. Maybe the other. I looked inside. Too dim. Biting my lip, taking a deep breath, reaching inside, this time gingerly, my fingers inched to the cool bottom. And there it was. Something hard. Metal. An L-shaped shaft with a hook on the end, a latch lifter attached to a ring sized for a man. A moment later, I had the key in my hand and was poking the shaft through the hole in one of the doors to lift the latch.

But then I stopped. Hadn't I already been gone too long? Shouldn't I put the key back and wait for another time? Another pretext? But who knows whether Eran would ever invite me back? The recipe could spread throughout the Empire in the meantime. Maybe I should have asked Judah to do it. But the truth is I wasn't sure what I could ask of him. So, despite the hammering in my chest, I turned the handles, pushed open the doors—they were heavy enough to challenge a Roman legion—and followed the thin stream of light that pointed into the room.

More than to welcome the light from the *impluvium*'s floating lamps, I left the doors ajar to monitor the conversation in the *triclinium*, already fortified by a second crater of wine. The darkness had begun to dissolve anyway as splashes of pearlescent light from the rising moon and writhing bursts from the sputtering torches worked their way through the chinks in the shutters. Ghostly shapes loomed out of the blue-black shadows and resolved themselves into more wood cabinets layered with more bric-a-brac; open shelves crammed with cracked, sour-smelling scrolls furry with dust; brooding ferns pluming over their pedestalled planters; and cushioned benches and wide tables piled high with waxed tablets and sheets of papyrus. And then, dominating the center of the room, I saw the massive marble-topped table that served as his desk.

Tingling with curiosity, I was eager to riffle through his sheets of papyrus, ransack his cabinets—each compartment was fitted with a lock—unfurl his scrolls—on second thought, they looked too old to warrant my attention—peel back the bench cushions, and upend the tables. Instead, with the warning of a moon already peeking above the grove's treetops, I tiptoed straight to his desk.

It too was smothered with junk, all reeking from his expensive fragrance—styluses, reed pens (most of them broken), sharpening knives, ink bottles, wax abacuses (the beads missing or scattered about), layers of opened scrolls that looked like his ledgers, a candelabrum (each arm a snake grasping a candle in its jaws), a dried puddle of wine, crumbs, sticks of wax—too higgledy-piggledy to tell me anything about a recently acquired scroll. Until I spotted a terracotta oil lamp. No wick. No cloying scent. But heavier than I expected. When I turned it upside down, nearly a dozen rings jangled out of the filling-hole. All were iron ring keys except one, a bronze seal ring, its stone an agate carved with an outline of a radiant sun the way a child would draw it.

I fingered each key. Surely one of these must open the compartment where he keeps the recipe, but which one? And which compartment? I must have been concentrating so keenly on the ring keys that I'd stopped listening to the voices in the *triclinium*. When had the hum of conversation stopped? I pricked up my ears.

Silence.

Then decisive heels clicking across the marble floor.

Drawing nearer.

Filling up the air.

Put the rings back, I told myself. But I froze like a statue.

Footsteps closer.

Fear compressed my chest.

Taking ownership of my hands, I jammed the rings back into the lamp.

The clang of metal reminded me.

My earring! Where'd I hide it?

Thoughts chasing thoughts.

My finger probed inside my *strophium*.

Fishing it out, my fingers curling around it, my nails digging into my palm so I wouldn't drop it, running toward the atrium only to collide with him just inside the threshold.

A dark tide spread upward from his neck, beyond his wig-less hairline, turning his birthmark so black it sucked in the light.

"I found it," I shrilled. Spreading open my fingers, I held up the earring. "It must have rolled under the doors."

His lips moved, but only a gag came out. Then, tightening his hands into fists, pumping his arms and stamping his feet, he released in a spray of acrid spittle a long, ear-scraping scream that reverberated through the house.

A wave of revulsion surged through my hollow belly.

"Out! Out!" he shrieked, pointing toward the entryway. Then he turned on his heel, his shoulders slumped, his body spent, and doddered back to the *triclinium*.

I lifted the lid and dropped the latch lifter into the *hydria*—I hoped the empty one—and bolted out the front doors a moment before they smacked shut. I ordered my knees to stop shaking, but they had a mind of their own.

Chapter 11

Sunday Morning

"SO TELL ME what we're shopping for this morning."

"Mouth rinse, natron, pomade, incense for our room, perfume, things like that. But I also have something else in mind."

Phoebe pursed her lips and shook her head.

"No, nothing about Eran's scroll. Well, hardly. As long as we're in Caesarea, aren't you just a little curious to see Bion?"

"Oh, Miriam, he's probably married with ten children by now."

"Well, it never hurts to say hello. Besides, maybe he can help me."

Phoebe and I were strolling southward on the *Cardo Maximus* toward the Forum. Having escaped the confines of our room, stuffy even at this early hour, we were eager to stretch our legs, inhale the raw sea breeze, and watch the gulls kite above the pounding surf. But our first stop would be a Roman-style cookshop for a breakfast of cinnamon tea, porridge, and figs.

We'd gone hardly a block before succumbing to the aromas of fresh barley rolls and grilled meats wafting out of Otho's *Thermopolium*, a modest cookshop on the northeast corner of the intersection. Phoebe went inside to claim a table while I eased in line to place our order at the streetside, marble-topped counter. Tradesmen, laborers, and produce vendors still chalky with the dust they'd gathered leading their mule-drawn carts through the countryside to the Northern Gate jabbered to each other in their spiky dialects as we each waited our turn. Meanwhile, I watched peddlers, astrologers, and everyone else with a portable business vie for a location close to the Forum and set up their pushcarts, tables, awnings, and umbrellas in preparation for a river of customers. A few minutes later, my eyes followed a rush of pigeons descending on an alley overflowing with garbage, and then, lowering my eyes, I saw a rat dart across the mica-grained, sun-flecked cobblestones into that same alley.

Phoebe beckoned me inside just as the counterman's son—he had the same underbite, sloping forehead, and pointed chin as the much-older Otho—delivered our order to the slightly sticky table. She'd arranged both chairs to face the street so we wouldn't have to look at the paintings lining the back wall, one more ribald than the next, and so we could watch the early morning sun pull back its shadows from the statues, columns, and arcades across the street.

"So, how are we going to find Bion?" Phoebe asked, turning to me with a challenge in her eyes.

"I figure when we're in the Forum, we can ask manuscript vendors whether they know a slave named Bion who repairs scrolls as a sideline. If that doesn't work, we can ask at the various synagogues for the name of the sandal-maker who bought him."

"And how do you think Bion could help?"

"Well, he might be able to teach me how to identify the provenance of a scroll, maybe by analyzing the papyrus or the ink, even the glue or the rods."

"You mean Eran's scroll."

When I nodded, Phoebe pursed her lips and shook her head again. "Miriam, you said—"

"I said 'hardly.' Our objective is to see whether we can find Bion, and if we do, I promise to ask him only about scrolls in general, nothing about Eran's."

I could tell Phoebe wasn't convinced. She crossed her arms, dropped her lids, gathered her lips into a tight circle, and waggled her head.

To tell the truth, I wasn't convinced either.

We finished our meal but slowly, Phoebe taking only the tiniest bite of her figs and gagging when she swallowed it as if it were a stone. At last she announced she was finished. We carved our way to the door through a knot of smiths and cutlers, butchers and tanners, fullers and coopers, and earned a scowl from the counterman for occupying the table so long—the line outside was already snaking around the block—but I simply smiled and waved goodbye.

Deferring our shopping in favor of searching for Bion, we entered a shop on the *Cardo Maximus* opposite the Forum. A terracotta plaque above the lintel read:

SPECIALIZING IN BUYING, SELLING, AND REPAIRING ANTIQUE MANUSCRIPTS.

Sure enough, showcases fronting the street displayed jars bearing such notable title-tags as *The Persians, Orestes, Antigone*, and rarest of all, a copy of Menander's *Dyskolos*, which Hector had made Phoebe and me read years ago along with the other three. While some bibliophiles sat on stools scrutinizing manuscripts as they hunched over a counter at the rear of the shop, clerks were assisting rounds of other customers even at this early hour. Phoebe meandered among the various tables stacked with blank scrolls, sheets of papyrus and parchment, ink, inkwells, bronze and reed *calami* or pens, sharpening knives, and styli. At the same time, I explored the wall cabinets filled with slender scrolls encased in parchment or linen sheaths and scanned the shelves laden with the works of contemporary writers like Thrasyllus of Mendes.

I approached the first available clerk, a slave with a bald, lopsided head. "I'm looking for someone named Bion, originally from Alexandria, who belongs to a sandal-maker and repairs scrolls. Do you know him?"

"I can't say I do, but my master's name is Bion, and he used to repair scrolls before teaching me the craft. Perhaps he knows the man you're looking for. He's in his office. I'll tell him you're asking about a namesake."

I couldn't be sure the man who emerged from behind the scrim at the back of the shop was Phoebe's Bion. I'd never met him, but he did have the gold-flecked eyes and rosy cheeks she'd told me about. Before the clerk had a chance to point me out though, this Bion glanced around the shop, and in a flash of wide-eyed recognition, uttered a cry of delight. Next, with a smile that split his cherubic face and cheeks that swallowed up his eyes, he leaped like a gazelle toward the writing supplies.

"Phoebe, my Phoebe. At last, my little Aphrodite has come." He sputtered the words as he gasped for breath. Then he took her trembling hand, kissed the palm, and, raising her chin with a gentle finger, looked deeply into her eyes. A blush raced up her neck, spread to the roots of her hairline, and on the way splashed her eyes with glitter.

He ushered her to a stool and asked a clerk to bring her some tea. Eyeing me, she held up her cupped hands to ask me whether I wanted some too, but I demurred with a wave of both palms and a waggle of my head. Then, pointing to the satchel, I mimed that I would attend to our shopping and return later. When she nodded, I turned to leave, looking back but once to see Phoebe gazing up at him, her lids narrowed, their bodies close, their movements in synchrony.

WHEN I RETURNED, the bald clerk dipped his lopsided head in a nod of recognition and held aside the scrim for me to enter a small, square office elegant in its tidy simplicity. The morning light slanting through the open shutters of the tall east window tinted the walls with a fresh, lemony finish and printed the window's mullions on the Oriental carpet. Stray beams polished the marble and bronze busts of the classical dramatists, poets, and philosophers who peered out from the niches and shelves above the waist-high marble-topped cabinets that lined the north and south walls.

Paintings of Alexandria hung on either side of the window, one of the Pharos Lighthouse in its nighttime glory, Poseidon poised above its cupola presiding with his trident over a placid sea, and the other, a view of our sprawling city from the summit of the Park of Pan. In the center of the room, Phoebe and Bion sat across from each other at a long rosewood table, their hands intertwined, their faces serene, their voices still cast in the pitch of intimate conversation.

They motioned for me to sit on the chair next to Phoebe. After the usual pleasantries and Bion's polite inquiry about the voyage—I skirted the issue of why we came to Caesarea—two clerks came in to serve us, the bald one with table linen draped over an arm that held a silver tray of Egyptian dates, Damascus figs, olives, barley cakes, filberts, and walnuts. The other—he had bright yellow eyes but no lashes—brought in an amphora of date juice, silver goblets, and Syrian glass plates. After they set the table and excused themselves, Bion invited Phoebe and me to help ourselves.

Following another polite interval accompanied by the ping of goblets and the gurgle of juice, Bion took a long sip, smacked his rosebud lips, and began the story of his good fortune in Caesarea.

"You may already know I left Alexandria eight years ago when the director of the Great Library sold me to Elisha ben Enoch, a Jewish sandal-maker and bibliophile from Caesarea. Ben Enoch bought me to catalog, repair, and most of all, to augment his collection of rare manuscripts through my contacts at the Library. Before too long, I was able to obtain several of Aristophanes's pungent satires, including my favorite *Lysistrata*, and a rare copy of *Oedipus the King*, which the Alexandrian scholars at the Library have certified as the canonical version."

Bion plucked a few filberts from the tray and munched on them thoughtfully, perhaps recalling those transactions or reviewing the chronology of his experiences in Caesarea. He took another sip and wiped his mouth on a napkin.

"Ben Enoch became wealthy as a sandal-maker for patrician women like Poppaea Sabina and Agrippina the Younger. He crafts their *soleae* from the softest pigskin leather, trims them with gold embroidery, Alexandrian beads, garnets, pearls, even emeralds, and adds thickness to the soles so his clients can flaunt their height along with their wealth. Ben Enoch's sandals are so prized they're sent to Rome regardless of the season on military transports carrying urgently needed supplies."

I lowered my chin to hide the smile puckering the corners

of my mouth. Playing across my mind's screen was the unbidden image of a score of fighting ships, the marines launching their projectiles, the archers taking aim, a host of arrows thrumming through the air, all to protect from pirates a fleet of military transports carrying nothing but sandals for Poppaea Sabina. I blinked away the image and bit my tongue just in time to forestall a fit of the giggles.

". . . and a generous master." Bion turned to look at me. "According to the Law of your people, which strictly regulates the treatment of slaves, perhaps because of your forefathers' enslavement in Egypt, he couldn't keep me longer than a year unless I agreed to be circumcised. So to continue in his household, I agreed, and from then on, he treated me more like a member of the family than a servant.

"Inasmuch as your Law permitted me to work no more than ten hours a day, six days a week, I hoped to earn the money to buy my freedom by repairing his friends' scrolls in my spare time. Can you imagine my amazement then when I learned that my having accepted the mark of your people meant I would be liberated after only six years? So two years ago, he gave me my quitclaim. But that wasn't all. He endowed me with a gift sufficiently generous for me to start a business of my own. Instead of the slave paying his master for his freedom, the Jewish master must pay his slave! No wonder my darling is so happy with you."

Nodding, he patted Phoebe's hand and, inhaling deeply, said to her in a voice grown hoarse, "Remember when you consoled me before I had to leave for Caesarea? You told me the ethical precepts of Judaism would spare me from the harshness of Roman slavery. I didn't realize then, my darling, how right you were."

Another rush of color rouged Phoebe's face.

"So," he said, shifting his gaze back to me, "with my master's gift added to what I'd managed to save, I was able to purchase this *bibliopōleion*, an inventory of rare manuscripts, and eventually these clerks. And with my connections to ben Enoch, his friends, and the director of the Great Library, I've been able to establish a thriving business."

He looked at Phoebe, and then, lifting his eyes, he smiled at the world.

We paused to enjoy the refreshments in earnest, and then I figured it was time for me to tell Bion why we'd come to Caesarea. So I put my tableware aside and pushed my chair back from the table.

"I became curious about the provenance of a particular scroll that's here in Caesarea. I'm hoping you can tell me about its origin. The problem is I'm having trouble getting hold of it, and even if I manage to borrow it, I don't think I could keep it long enough to bring it to you."

That put it mildly.

"Actually," he said, "I need only a panel, not even the entire scroll. And it would be simple enough for you to detach and re-attach the panel yourself."

A spark of hope burned through the fog in my brain. If I removed a panel near the end of the scroll, providing the scroll is bulky enough, Eran might not notice it was even missing.

Bion explained that I could separate a panel with the caustic soap made from tallow and ashes, the kind imported from Gaul for ladies who want to be blondes or redheads. I'd make a mild solution of soap and water and apply it along both seams of the panel to dissolve the glue. The technique he uses is to take the cotton fibers sold in an apothecary shop (the kind used to absorb the poisons from an open wound), soak them in the solution, squeeze out the excess liquid, lay the fibers along the panel seams, and let the solution migrate into the seams overnight. In the morning, he said, I'd be able to peel apart the panel. All I'd have to do then is dry the panel for a few hours under pressure to prevent its edges from dimpling.

Re-gluing the panel, he said, is just as simple. I'd make a paste of flour, boiling water, and a sprinkle of vinegar, let the paste thicken for a day, apply it in a narrow strip along each vertical edge of the panel, use the rest of the cotton fibers to soak up any excess, press the panel back in place, flatten the seams with a mallet, and then let the scroll dry in the sun for a day.

With that, he got up from the table and fetched a mallet from the workbench alongside the scrim. Next he went to a polished acacia cabinet under the busts of Aristotle, Plato, and Homer and filled glass vials with what he guessed would be more than enough flour, vinegar, caustic soap, and cotton fibers to do the job. And then he gave me one last item from the workbench.

"Use this glass globe of water to magnify the grain of fibers on the panel when you re-glue it. Make sure it lines up with the grain on the adjacent panels. Then your repair will be invisible."

I crammed the mallet, globe, and the four vials into the satchel, already brimming with the day's purchases. With my heartfelt thanks and a plan of action, I was ready to head back to the inn.

As we were about to leave, Bion rushed over to grasp Phoebe's hand once more and ask when he could see her again. To avoid intruding on their parting, I made my way to the street. A team of *pedisequi*, the slaves who trot ahead of and alongside their master's litter, was splitting the crowd with long bamboo canes to make way for the gigantic bearers and the litter itself, a polished bronze cabin gleaming in the midday sun, its lacey curtains drawn apart, probably for the occupant to view the bustle about the Forum. Distracted for the moment by the contents shifting in the satchel, I rummaged through the packages to make sure the wax seals on the vials were secure. Not a moment later, Phoebe was beside me.

As she watched the litter pass, her mouth hinged open, a look of horror overtook her, and her body began to shake.

"What is it?" I asked.

She was slow to answer. "I thought for a jarring moment I saw someone from Alexandria in that litter, but now I'm sure I was mistaken."

"Who was it, Phoebe?"

As if her throat had clamped shut, she shook her head and would say no more.

Chapter 12

Sunday Afternoon

JUDAH AND I stared at each other across an embroidered linen tablecloth in the dining room of The Three Graces. The specter of a rebuke loomed in the air. Outlined by the light that slanted through the window behind him and curved around his wreath of curls, he looked at me with narrowed eyes, his brow creased with anger, his fingers drumming on the edge of the table.

"Thank you for bringing my himation," I said, tucking it into my satchel, trying to set an amiable tone. "When I couldn't find it, I realized I must have left it at Eran's."

But my expression of gratitude didn't work. He shook his head and raked his hands through his hair, a gesture I'd learned to read as exasperation.

"What on earth possessed you to sneak into his study like that? I warned you he's hard to get to know and has a volatile temper besides. But instead of taking the time to earn his trust, you abused his hospitality and violated his privacy."

I could tell by his measured diction he was making a Herculean effort to keep his voice calm.

"And, believe me, your losing an earring had about as much credibility as the word of a ship captain. What were you thinking of?" His tone had become shriller.

Right then I was thinking he sounded just like Noah. But I knew better than to start an argument. So I sat with my fingers laced, hardly listening, instead scouring my brain for a convincing explanation.

"I think Eran's in danger, and we're the only ones who can protect him."

He squinted and thrust out his neck like a turtle, so I continued.

"Look, as far as we know, only our League of Alchemists has been working on the perfection of metals and only you and Saul on copper in particular. We need to find out whether Eran has an authentic recipe for the perfection of copper. If he does, he needs to be warned. He and his associates—and that would include you, Judah—could be accused of cheating his most prominent client, the procurator himself. For that alone, Alexander would eagerly impose the *summum supplicium* personally. He could certainly afford any depreciation in the value of the pieces Eran wrought for him, but what about the raised eyebrows, the wagging tongues, the sly nods, the careless snickers, the twitches of amusement, and the scoffs behind palm-covered mouths mocking him for his folly?"

Right then I imagined Alexander draped in the exquisite robes of his office, his hair dressed with an exotic pomade, the scent floating over the voluptuous furnishings in the basilical hall of the Upper Palace, his sycophants drinking in the sweet fragrance. His countenance chiseled in marble, his eyes fixed on Eran, he pronounces sentence with the utmost calm in a soft, even voice: "Of course, you must die. I have yet to decide how, only that the manner will be neither quick nor painless." Then, turning away from his prisoner, the slightest smile plays at the corners of his mouth.

"And that would be only the beginning. Need I remind you of the fifty-day agricultural strike in Galilee after that Roman deputy from Syria insisted on installing graven images in Tiberias? The barley corn crop was so precious that the deputy had to relent. And before that, the five days and nights of protest right here in Caesarea? Even Pilate's threat to hack the demonstrators to pieces couldn't coerce them into accepting Caesar's image inside Jerusalem. Imagine the mighty power of Rome yielding to these scruffy, unarmed rebels! So Alexander would gladly use Eran's arrest as an excuse to incite a pogrom that could make the one in Alexandria look like a family squabble."

Fear hardened the creases in Judah's brow.

"We need to protect Eran. And we need to find out as soon as possible where the recipe came from and the extent it's been disseminated so we can, in obedience to G-d's will, forestall its spread beyond the Seed of Abraham. You sent me the letter more than two months ago. Who knows how long Eran had the recipe before that?"

I wasn't about to admit I might be responsible for Eran's having gotten the recipe in the first place. I was still too ashamed. Besides, I'd already gone through so much to return the League's scrolls and cover up my lie.

Instead of drumming his fingers, Judah's hands gripped the edge of the table. He waited a few seconds before speaking, and when he did, I heard a quaver in his voice.

"So, tell me, what can we do?"

"Well, before doing anything, we need to find out whether the recipe could be authentic. But even if it's not, I want to track down its provenance. Phoebe has an old friend who owns a *bibliopōleion* right here on the *Cardo Maximus* opposite the Forum. He says he'd need just a single panel. Of course, I didn't tell him anything about Eran's, but he said he'd be willing to look at anything I bring him."

"So you want Phoebe's friend to look at a panel from Eran's scroll?"

"Yes, but I'm afraid. Do you know whether Eran's been experimenting with the recipe? If he has, he might notice a missing panel, even if it's near the end of the scroll."

"I don't think so. I've looked around. He doesn't stock cinnabar, orpiment, pyrites of silver, uncorrupted urine, horse manure, white alum, oxymel, or any of the other reagents we use. Not in his house or his shop. And I haven't seen any of the tubes, filters, and furnaces we use to heat our waters and condense their vapors."

"In that case, let's do it." I dipped into the satchel and put the mallet, globe, and vials on the table. Pointing to each item while mentally ticking off each step, I repeated Bion's directions and added my own. "But be sure to re-glue the scroll after you remove the panel. Don't wait until I bring the panel back. Then, if Eran happens to want to study the scroll in the meantime, it will at least look intact. And another thing: Work on the scroll at night, while Eran's asleep. Then you can dry it in the sun the next day and return it that night so it will have been missing only that one day. Your real problem will be finding the scroll."

I told him about all the keys in the terracotta lamp on Eran's desk, that I believed one of them must open the compartment where he keeps the scroll. The other scrolls, the ones stacked on the open shelves, were too caked with dust to be the object of our quest.

"Eran hides the key to his study in one of the *hydriae* in the atrium. I just don't remember which one. In the other, I suspect he keeps a snake, perhaps an asp—"

"Oh, that's ridiculous—"

"Judah, you'd better listen to me. Eran's a man who guards his privacy. Poke inside the *hydria* with a stick or shine a beam of light inside before you reach in."

"Okay, I'll do whatever you say." He nodded slowly, his shoulders relaxing, his hand covering and patting mine. "What's more, I'm sorry. You must know I've been annoyed with you for coming to Caesarea and especially angry for your behavior at Eran's, but now I see you're doing so much for him. Really for both of us. Please forgive me, Miriam."

When I heard him speak my name in such a tender whisper, I felt that familiar longing. And when I saw his mouth soften, I imagined him covering me with his silky lips, his tongue bringing me to the brink of ecstasy. But my sweet fantasy lasted but an instant.

"Miriam! There you are," Phoebe gasped as she rushed into the dining room. "I couldn't find your himation anywh—"

At that moment, she must have noticed Judah's hand on mine because she raised her brows in a fluster and clamped her hand over her mouth. Then, sliding it away and dropping her eyes, she turned to him. "Oh, I didn't mean to interrupt."

"That's all right," he mumbled as he got up. "I have things to do anyway."

With that, he packed the items from Bion into the leather purse secured to his belt and left in a cloud of preoccupation. And I wondered too late whether I'd just sent him on a dangerous mission to right a wrong that belonged to me.

Chapter 13

Wednesday Morning

THE PUBLIC DINING room of The Three Graces was abuzz that morning with the chatter of tourists and the bustle of waiters shouldering silver trays laden with olives and goat cheese, pomegranates and blackberries, biscuits spiced with ground locusts, and mugs of watered curds flavored with honey. Anticipating Judah's arrival after receiving a message from him yesterday to meet him here for breakfast, I sat at a table set for two with alabaster crockery. A shaft of clear morning sunlight warmed a swath on the starched linen cloth before spilling onto the pantheon of deities tessellated on the floor.

With Phoebe out and about, off first to the bathhouse and then to a certain *bibliopōleion* on the *Cardo Maximus*, I passed the time sipping tea and letting its steam soothe my face while I surveyed the attire of the women staying here. A pair of Judean matrons sat at the table to my right, probably a mother and daughter, one being elderly, her forehead corrugated, her eyes webbed. Their heads were covered with long shawls, one end swept up to veil all below their eyes, the other draped across the opposite shoulder. Their amply cut, ankle-length woolen tunics were tied with a wide embroidered sash and fastened with brass buckles, clasps, and pins. And their feet, dressed in goat leather *soleae*, peeked out from the fringed mantles that draped loosely over their tunics.

I was about to focus on the horsy matron at the table across from me—her hair was dyed an unconvincing carroty red and coiled into an elaborate tower—when Judah rushed in breathless, his face flushed, his eyes rimmed with fatigue.

"Miriam, I thought he'd never leave." Judah hooked his

foot around the leg of the chair and dragged it out from under the table. Then he flopped down and plunked his elbows over the arms of the chair before hunching forward to catch his breath.

"What are you talking about?"

"Eran," said Judah, his speech choppy, his breath still fluttering like the wings of a trapped bird. "Didn't get to remove the panel until last night. Wanted to put the scroll out to dry this morning. Had to wait so long for him to leave, to feed whatever lives in that *hydria*. He dropped in a toad, kicking and squirming—first one jumped right out—keeps a knot of them in a terrarium . . . a rustle, a few thumps, the *hydria* shifting on the polished floor. Then a hush."

"Be careful, Judah. It would be just like Eran to switch them around. Check each time you want to get the key."

"Oh, Miriam. I'll admit he's peculiar, but he's not a monster." His voice dropped to a whisper. "Anyway, here's the panel, the penultimate one in the scroll."

He'd rolled it around a thick dowel and wrapped it in a linen sheath that I could slip into my satchel.

"But that's not all."

My body stiffened.

"When I left you and Phoebe on Sunday, I went to a stationery store for the dowel, a textile shop for the sheath, and an apothecary shop for a light tincture of opium. I added the tincture to the wine he drinks with his evening meal. I didn't think he'd notice the bitterness—and he didn't—because he's only just started scenting his wine with jasmine, the latest of his Roman affectations. I myself, feigning a headache, refused the wine and went to bed early—not that I could sleep—but I drank a full goblet of water anyway to guarantee I'd wake up long before morning if I happened to doze off."

"So what happened?" I said, rolling my hands forward in tight circles to get him to speed up his story. "Did you have a chance to look over the recipe?" My head was throbbing by then, but I tried to muster whatever patience I could.

"Yes, I read the entire recipe, but I barely finished it before dawn. First I had to get into his study. I did like you said. I probed inside each *hydria* with a stick. In the first one, something yanked back. I was so startled, I almost got giddy. But I heard the clang of the latch lifter when I probed inside the other one, and just to be safe, I used the stick to fish it out."

At this rate, we'd be eating lunch before he finished his story.

"So, did the recipe look familiar?"

"Wait a minute. I'm getting to that."

But before he got around to answering, I had to endure a detailed account of how he matched each key in the oil lamp—he said there were ten—to each of the various locked compartments in Eran's cabinets—also ten—and how he tried each key in turn until he found the scroll on the eighth try.

"Now here's the strangest thing," he said, hinging forward and narrowing his eyes in perplexity.

I moved in close.

"The recipe is Saul's and mine all right, no more and no less, down to our list of unsuccessful trials and the names of the Alexandrian merchants who supply us with reagents. Even Kimon's on the list. Remember him? The old man with the harelip who has a shop on the Canopic Way just west of the Palace of Justice? The one who imports copper for us from Mainland Greece?"

I sat behind a stone mask while a flock of nightmarish creatures took turns puncturing my innards with a spike.

"Of course, the recipe has errors, some based on carelessness as if the scribe was in a hurry and some based on misinterpreting our symbols. In one place, the scribe muddles the directions for a procedure by misreading our symbol for mercury as a reference to the planet.

"But, yes, the recipe is definitely Saul's and mine copied by a scribe unfamiliar with our lore. So how on earth did our work end up here? And more important, how can we protect Eran?"

We gaped at each other while exchanging the foul breath of dread.

"Judah, it may be more complicated than that. Eran's scroll

may not be the only rogue copy."

"I'm just glad Saul isn't alive to see this."

Just then the polite cough of an anxious waiter interrupted the mute screams of my conscience.

Chapter 14

Early Wednesday Afternoon

WITH THE PANEL tucked away in my satchel, I stepped outside The Three Graces into the afternoon light and strode southward toward Bion's shop, treading on the skirts of my swiftly moving shadow and the lacey shade of the needle-leafed trees lining the *cardo*. Bion's bald clerk, once again dipping his lopsided head in a nod of recognition, escorted me directly into the office where I joined Phoebe and Bion as they were finishing a lunch of pita, lentils, wild greens, dried fruit, and ginger tea.

My head spun like a potter's wheel, but I managed to control the fever of my impatience until the yellow-eyed clerk glided in and cleared the table. Then, as soon as he left, I took out the panel and handed it to Bion. Shifting his weight, he pivoted out of his chair and scooted over to his workbench where he planted his feet firmly astride the stool and examined the panel with a glass globe, this one much larger than the one he'd lent me.

I can't say whether his inspection took a minute or an hour, only that I nibbled on my cuticles, waiting for each brittle moment to pass. Sometimes he'd turn and lift the panel to catch a beam of light from the window, but most of the time he hunched over the workbench, his brow furrowed, his eyes riveted to the globe as he shifted it from one section of the panel to another, his body otherwise motionless. Finally, nodding with certainty, he looked up, pulled in a deep breath, and spoke in an authoritative voice.

"Based on the handwriting, I'd say the copy was made by a man, definitely a professional scribe despite some uneven strokes, and based on the fact that he wrote on the recto side of the papyrus, I'd say the panel had never been washed and re-used.

"The ink is the usual blend of lampblack, gum, and water, but the scribe must have been in a hurry when he added the water because in some spots, the ink ran and left gray splotches, and in others, the ink dried prematurely and left black nubs."

Phoebe glowed with pride.

"And look here," he said, handing me the globe and pointing to nicks on the panel. "Another indication he worked in haste is that he allowed the point of his *calamus* to get dull before re-sharpening it. You can see where he scratched the papyrus with the blunted point.

"But most important to pinpointing its provenance, the panel, judging by its smoothness, is made of the finest center-cut Egyptian papyrus, probably from one of the factories along Lake Mareotis that serves an elite clientele, definitely not from the huge papyrus beds growing here by the Jordan."

This time the nightmarish creatures seized me from behind and grabbed me by the throat with their claws. I wondered whether my tongue was swelling and my eyes bulging, but I felt only a runaway heartbeat and a numbness all over my face. I elbowed the beasts behind me to loosen their grip, blinked my eyes to chase them away, and instead recalled a telling excursion on a long-ago summer day.

Amram had taken Noah, Binyamin, and me on a daytrip to watch the papyrus-makers in one of the factories on the marshy banks of Lake Mareotis. Despite the stretch of nearly a dozen years, I could hear the gravelly jabber of the dusty, walnut-faced workers splitting the plant stems into strips and the flinty voice of a young Noah when he touched the sheets made from only the center strips: "When I grow up, that's the only kind of papyrus I'll buy. I won't write on anything but the smoothest sheets."

I didn't need Bion to tell me anything else. Just as I'd feared, the copy must have come from Noah's house. If I could only find out how Eran got it, then I might be able to check its spread.

All I needed was a plan.

Chapter 15

Late Wednesday Afternoon

THE PANEL WAS once again tucked away in my satchel, but I was too restless to return to the inn, so I asked Phoebe to ramble about the Forum with me. Despite the din, the swelter, the drone of flies, the scamper of rats, the squirts of pigeons, the stench of baking ordure, and the reek of raw meat dripping puddles of blood, I longed to lose myself in its zest. Where else could I finger the coolness of lapis, jade, turquoise, and carnelian; taste the bitterness of chicory and the sourness of sorrel; crush the leaves of coriander in my palm; and inhale the spicy aromas of frankincense, cardamom, pepper, and cassia? Where else could I chart my future with a Roman astrologer, buy a spell from an Egyptian witch, heed the incantations of a Babylonian soothsayer, or catch the harangue of a Cynic?

Heat ricocheted off the creamy stone façades of the banks, law courts, and city offices housed within the block-long precinct and spread a shimmer on the merchants' wagons, traders' stalls, moneychangers' tables, and green grocers' carts clustered around the shops. But with the sun sliding down the southwestern sky, the cruel heat of midday had loosened its grip. And so the regulars had resumed their rhythm of buying, selling, bartering, hawking, extorting, and swindling in a variety of languages: the peasants trading their oil in Aramaic, the *agoranomoi* checking the vendors' scales in Greek, and the *coactoris* collecting the emperor's taxes in Latin.

We crossed the *cardo* and entered the Forum, sidling through the line to the tinker's booth, paddling against a sea of shoppers and pickpockets, freedmen and slaves, idlers and peddlers, old soldiers and painted whores. Finally caught in the tide, we zigzagged around the wobbly tents and awning-sheltered barrows of snake charmers, seers, magicians, wizards, and sorcerers. Buoyed along, pressed against sweaty bodies, we spilled into a marketplace artery only to lurch back on trampled toes to make way for a cavalryman patrolling the Forum in his crested helmet, leather cuirass, and red cloak. Wearing the mask of Roman authority, his features hard around young eyes, he was flanked by a pair of infantrymen, their swords hanging from their belts, their hobnail boots scraping the pavement as they prodded the crowd with their long staffs.

Ducking into the inky shade of a narrow alleyway, pulling Phoebe in behind me, I turned an instant later when I heard the savage howl of a stray dog and saw its yellow eyes aflame, its hackles up, its monstrous fangs bared. It lunged, its drool flying from its purple tongue and pendant lips as it nipped and then gnawed at the foreleg of the cavalryman's horse. Raising a plume of dust, switching its tail, the horse reared up on its haunches, neighing and blowing and snorting in fright. Then, amid the drumming of its hooves and the ragged screams of the startled crowd, an elderly woman, the very same Judean matron from the inn, scuttled in front of me.

A moment later she lay on the pavement spurting a fountain of blood from a hole in her chest, the handle of a dagger protruding like a tongue from the mouth of her wound. As the flow from her chest slackened to a trickle, I heard a brittle gurgle, and then she was still. Soon the sour smell of excrement and the rusty stink of blood rose up from the pavement.

Looking up, I saw the back of a fully-mantled figure, probably a man judging by the gait and posture, melt into the crowd.

The cavalryman dropped to his haunches and leaned over the old woman's body. Her companion, half mad, wailed beside him, her head bowed and shoulders shaking as her metallic sobs tore through the Forum. He pulled out the short, curved brass dagger, examined it, and declared through stiff lips that the crime was the work of the *Sicarii*. Holding up the *sica*, he asked the dazed witnesses in a guttural Latin for any information about the attack.

"Miriam, it looked like the killer was aiming for you."

"Oh, Phoebe, that's preposterous. Who even knows I'm here?"

Before I had a chance to wonder why the *Sicarii* had singled out that old woman, I noticed the emblem on the *sica*'s handle, a crude outline of a radiant sun.

Despite the heat, I began to shiver.

Chapter 16

Friday (Shabbat) Evening

"I UNDERSTAND THE *Sicarii* target Jews who are traitors to our people, especially the Greek Jews who collaborate with Rome. So why do you suppose they murdered that poor old woman?"

I posed the question to Eran in his *triclinium* as he and Jabin, Judah and I took our places, goblets in hand, on the padded dining couches. Awaiting the first course of a festive Shabbat dinner, I watched the flames of the candelabra reach for the vaulted ceiling, their sparks bursting into needles of light that showered over the lamp stands.

When Judah had relayed Eran's invitation, I was incredulous. How could Eran invite me back after he found me snooping in his study? But Judah insisted the invitation was sincere, that Eran welcomed the opportunity to make amends for having lost his temper, that Shabbat was after all a time for peace and reconciliation, and that given the chance, Eran would surely warm up to me. So for Judah's sake, I consented. Besides, with nothing more to learn from the scroll itself—Judah returned it intact to its compartment last night—the easiest way for me to find out how Eran got it and the only way I could think of right then was to ask him.

Eran pursed his lips, but instead of responding to my question about the murdered woman, he rambled on about the economic effect of the Roman occupation on different classes of Judeans.

"My dear young lady, we in Judea regard all non-Jews as unclean and keep apart from them. But to us, the Romans are the most abominable heathens of all. So their very presence is an affront to us. Some, like the Sadducees, who have been drawn from the old wealthy aristocratic families, are either resigned to their rule or accept it because it provides us with domestic stability and protection from foreign invasions, conditions that I need not remind you translate into profits."

Eran lifted his goblet to signal one of the houseboys to refill it.

"But the more rigorously religious like the Pharisees, who pride themselves on their piety and rigid interpretation of the Law, condemn those supporting the established order as pagan sympathizers or worse yet, as traitors.

"The peasants likewise bitterly oppose the occupation. The economy of the Romans has impoverished them. They continue to work the plots they once owned, but now as tenant farmers, they must buy back their own produce. They are the ones who lead the resistance and assassinate traitors in the name of freedom and for the cause of Judean independence."

"But the woman—"

"My dear," he said with a flick of his hand, "I suspect her husband killed her for committing adultery, and yes, he's probably a member of the *Sicarii*. You say she was staying at your inn? He must have caught her there with another man."

His lips stretched in a knowing smile.

"But she hardly seemed the type. She was elderly and modestly dressed. And she was in the company of another woman. Besides, the bedrooms in the inn are exclusively for—"

"Don't play games with me, young lady. I'm not so naïve as my brother. All women are seductresses. She deserved to die for that alone." Eran was propped up on his left elbow. Pointing at me with his right hand, he stabbed the air with his index finger when he said the word "die."

The movement shifted his wig.

I could see his port-wine stain darkening.

"But if her husband wanted her punished, couldn't he have appealed to the religious courts?"

Eran took a sip from his goblet. Then drinking more greedily, he drained the cup and, swiveling his head, signaled for more.

"Why should he bother with the Sanhedrin?" Rills of wine leaked down his chin and onto his *synthesis*. "The procurator can quash the death sentence for a religious crime anyway. And he probably would have. Didn't I just get finished telling you the Romans are heathens? They disrespect our Law. Their depravity is boundless—"

"But the woman—"

"The woman? Don't forget, I've had experience with women. They—and that includes you, my dear—know how to tempt."

A glance across the table showed me a white-faced Judah raking his hands through his hair.

"Didn't Judah's mother seduce my father? That whore stole him from his family, drove my mother hopelessly insane, and deprived me of all I ever wanted, a father's love. Instead, Judah was reared as if he were the legitimate son and I, the bastard.

"And haven't you too come into my house like a whore?" His voice trembled with rage. "Intent on stealing not just my recipe but my brother as well? Provoking my temper and then using my helpless outbursts to poison him against me? So don't tell me about women. Every one of you is a whore."

"Yes, I can see you've suffered at the hands of selfish women, but in the process, you've learned so much. I must say I admire you for that."

His brow softened with my flattery, so I figured why stop.

"And you mentioned the recipe. You're right again. It's of great interest to me, but not its contents, only how you acquired it. My guess is it came from Alexandria."

A snarl escaped from his throat before turning into a savage laugh.

"There you go again, trying to trick me into revealing how I got it, so you can get a copy for yourself. But no. It's mine, all mine."

Then, turning to Judah, he continued. "And as long as I have it, I'm powerful, more powerful than you, my mealy-mouthed, lover-boy brother, and that oversexed liar-of-a-father of ours. May his wasted soul and that of his filthy whore be burning at this very moment in the fires of Gehenna."

He leaned in close to me. His fetid breath and the sour wine that reeked from his pores coated me with his stink. Then he dropped his voice to a conspiratorial whisper.

"By the way, do you spread your legs for my brother like his mother did for my spineless father? Does he give you what you want? Are his thrusts powerful enough to satisfy you, or is his manhood a sack of limp flesh?"

I could only stare while a tangy stream coated the back of my throat.

"No matter," he said triumphantly. "I have the recipe."

Then his voice swelled to a furious thunder, a shower of his spittle sprayed the table, and his port-wine stain deepened to a satiny black.

"And you will never—do you hear me, slut?—you will never gain possession of it."

Once again, I donned my stone mask, this time to hide my consternation. Still, there was something so pathetic, even defenseless, about him. Judah got up, wordlessly circled the table to my couch, and tapped my elbow to signal we were leaving. Padding silently into the atrium, past the mahogany bench where we picked up our himations, we escaped into the calm Shabbat night.

AS JUDAH WALKED me back to the inn, he put a protective arm around my waist as if to shield me from further insults. I slowed my steps to fall more deeply into his embrace while imagining we were sweethearts in search of a deserted beach. Occasionally, I'd dare a glance in his direction to see a shaft of moonlight illuminate his profile. Neither of us spoke until we passed the little synagogue and heard the chants of Shabbat sweeten the breeze that drifted in from the sea.

"Judah, I'm afraid your brother is mad, absolutely mad, probably suffering from the same mania that consumed his mother."

He stopped in his tracks and, turning toward me, withdrew

his arm from my waist.

"No, I don't think so. I'm sure it was just the wine. You haven't seen the temperate side of him."

"But you heard what he said about you. I'm afraid for you if you continue to stay in his house. Suppose he discovers you tampered with his scroll. Maybe he's set a trap we're not even aware of. I'm telling you, he's dangerous. Not only that, he himself would be in danger if others find out he has that recipe. And given his volatility, I don't think he'll be able to keep that secret much longer. I tell you, I'm afraid for him, for you, for all of us."

"Oh, Miriam, stop exaggerating."

Did I hear him right? I felt the sting of angry tears behind my eyes.

"How can you dismiss your brother's suspiciousness? Didn't you hear how he accused that poor woman of adultery? And what about his conviction that all women are whores?" Was my voice getting shrill, or was it just the way it sounded inside my head above the roar of rushing blood?

"Look, he drank too much wine. Understandably. He was nervous about your coming to dinner, not sure about your sanity given how you behaved last time but willing to take a chance anyway. You're really quite obsessed with that scroll. And then the way you browbeat him about that woman as if he were responsible for her death. I can't say I blame him for getting upset."

"Are you saying I'm responsible for his behavior?"

"I'm saying he's been hurt by women through no fault of his own. By virtue of his mother's illness, he was neglected. And to be fair, my mother and I did take up a lot of our father's time. To make matters worse, our father lied to him repeatedly about his absences, and Eran knew it. And finally, regardless of his charitable acts, the most pious Jews still reject him as unclean because of his port-wine stain."

"Well, that would explain why he envies you."

"Yes, and his envy would be justified."

"And why, in a jealous rage, he could hurt you."

His voice softened. "Look, Miriam, the least I can do for him now is befriend him. That's why I'm here and why you mustn't stand in my way."

How beautiful he looked standing there under the glittering net of Shabbat stars.

"All right. So what should I do?"

I watched his gaze thicken.

"I want you to show him respect. Admire his work. Go to his shop. Even buy something to take back to Alexandria. If you're afraid of him, take Phoebe along, but please, Miriam, do this for me. Meet him halfway."

I'd hoped for a different answer, but try as I might, I couldn't frame a sensible objection.

Chapter 17

Sunday Morning

THIS TIME AS WE walked toward the Forum, Phoebe and I resisted the savory aromas that seasoned the air around Otho's *Thermopolium* in favor of getting our visit to Eran's shop over with. Besides, I was in no mood to deal with another scowl from the counterman.

The rickety stalls of portable commerce were already fringing the Forum. Shoppers swarmed around them, shouting in Aramaic, Greek, and Latin above the call of conjurers, the haggle of vendors, the clop of hooves, and the rumble of wooden-wheeled pushcarts bullying their way over the cobblestones. Beyond the wall of noise, I caught the shimmer of the statues, columns, and arcades lining the Forum, their edges sharper than ever in the painfully bright morning sun.

Our plan was to cut through the Forum to get to Eran's shop on the *Decumanus Maximus*. Perhaps on the way I'd purchase a peace offering. Another figurine or primitive mask, censer or marble plaque, silk cushion or allegorical tapestry. He couldn't seem to get enough of them. As we did last Wednesday, we entered the Forum near the tinker's booth and followed our elongated shadows toward the narrow alleyway. Nothing marked the spot where the old woman died except a tuft of horse dung.

We were about to look in a textile shop, Phoebe trailing behind me with our satchel, when its door yawned open, and a lean, pockmarked face peered out from a long, hooded black silk cloak. The tips of the wearer's grayish teeth hooked over his lower lip as he swiveled his head right and left before striding off, his right arm sheltering a plain but distinctly new linen satchel. As if I'd stepped into a viper's nest, I recoiled and turned to warn Phoebe. Too late. I could tell by the set of her jaw that she'd seen him too.

"Phoebe, you recognize him?"

"That's Noah's scribe," she said, pointing with her chin, "the one who used to bring documents to your father. And by his demeanor, I'd say he's up to no good. He's the one I thought I saw in that fancy litter outside Bion's shop last Sunday. But then I figured I must be mistaken, that I was getting mixed up between Alexandria and Caesarea. Besides, who'd have guessed he'd be parading around like a notable?"

"Yes, Drakon's come up in the world since Noah fired him. Now he's Alexander's head scribe."

"Well, something about him has always reminded me of a spider building a web one deathly strand at a time. Maybe it's because when he'd wait for your father, he'd ask for Kastor. Remember him, the secretary with the clubfoot? The one your father sold to the Public Records Office in Alexandria? The two of them would whisper in Latin behind cupped hands, about what I don't know, but then in a rhythmic sequence, Drakon would clap Kastor's shoulder, rub his palms together, and strut off, flicking his poisonous tongue across his lower lip."

"Did you know he blames me for getting him fired? One day soon after, he encountered me in the *Bruchium* quarter near Aspasia's. He leaned into me with a flood of curses and crowed that he'd be leaving for Caesarea to work for the procurator where he pledged—and these were his exact words—'to stir up trouble against the likes of you and your smarmy race.' I realized then how deeply hatred can burrow into someone's soul.

"Anyway, whatever he's up to, I'll bet he'll be using that new bag. Did you see how tightly he hugged it to his body?"

"Miriam, listen. He might recognize you, but he'd never recognize me, especially since he doesn't know we're even in Caesarea. Let me follow him right now, just inside the Forum, no farther, just to see where he's headed."

"I don't know. Remember the matron who was killed right

here? It could be dangerous, more so with the crowds thickening at this hour. And Drakon himself is dangerous. He's a snoop, Phoebe. That's why Noah fired him." I didn't mention that Drakon had had access to Noah's stock of center-cut papyrus. And as Alexander's scribe, Drakon could have made Eran's acquaintance at the Palace, and in spite of the danger, offered him a chance to buy the recipe right under Alexander's nose.

"Oh, please let me, Miriam. I'll be careful, I promise." She tugged at my arm while her eyes glittered with an impish excitement. "It's not like I'll lose my way in this impenetrable darkness," she teased.

Was I making too much of a simple stroll in the Forum? Seeing Drakon here in Caesarea was like opening the door to a labyrinth I couldn't enter. But Phoebe could. How dangerous could it be?

"On one condition, Phoebe. Well, really three. First that you drape my himation around your head so the end veils your face. Second, that you follow him in the Forum but not a step beyond, and third, that you come back to our room immediately afterward. I'll be waiting there for you as soon as I've finished with Eran."

Wrapping her in my himation and then in my embrace, I whispered in a tone more resolute than I felt, "Now hurry, or we'll lose track of him."

A glee-spiked squeal bubbled up from Phoebe's throat while I wondered whether Judah had been right—that I'd become obsessed with Eran's accursed scroll.

A SINGSONG GREETING welcomed me into Eran's shop as if I were a long-lost friend. At first I couldn't see him, eclipsed as he was by every sort of garish presentation piece that could be crammed into the shadowy space that was both his showroom and workshop. Every horizontal surface (shelf, table, stool, display counter, even the floor) was strewn with lamp stands or censers. Or jammed with figurines atop platters or cutlery inside craters. Or stacked with oil lamps against busts or trays across toppled candelabra. As I looked around, a horde of suspicious statues seemed to inch toward me as if to trap me in their claustrophobic chaos. If any taxonomy structured their arrangement, be it size, metal, or forging technique, none was apparent.

I heard a jingle and a ping as he set down his tools. Then, cutting a path to the door, he called to an errand boy to bring us some goat cheese and a jug of honey-sweetened water. Inclining his head in my direction, which I took to mean I should follow him into the bowels of the shop, he led me to a display counter, where he swept away a tower of polished bronze hand mirrors—several crashed to the floor where he left them reverberating like cymbals—and unloaded a dozen candlesticks from a pair of stools. All the while, he mentioned nothing about last Shabbat but commented instead in a rapid stream on the state of his business as if we'd been conversing for hours.

"Gold is more scarce than ever, so I work mostly in silver, brass, and bronze. Even iron," he said, pointing to a bizarre lamp stand wrought in the shape of a feeding vulture. "I still import gold from Spain, but mainly for the procurator. Among other things, I craft the medallions he presents to the victorious gladiators. But piracy threatens the gold supply even when the ingots are carried by military transport.

"For instance, take this statuette I'm casting for a client who lives near the South Gate. Years ago I would have insisted on working in nothing less than gold, but I'm willing now, at least temporarily, to use brass. With my reputation as a master goldsmith, I'm offered commissions from as far away as Joppa, even Jerusalem, but," he said with a shrug and open palms, "many of those I have to decline if they insist on gold."

I certainly wasn't about to discuss the scarcity of gold with him. Still, I was curious about the source of his brass. Was he importing it from Cyprus? Nearly as valuable as gold, wouldn't that supply also be threatened, this time by those notorious pirates along the Anatolian coast, the very outlaws who destroyed my maternal grandparents' shipping business? Or was he instead melting down Roman coins and military equipment? Probably not. Most Judeans would refuse to buy anything made of Roman brass. So he must be manufacturing it himself. What's more, his brass has a distinctive golden color, which must mean he's using more than the usual proportion of calamine (zinc ores). Anyway, I didn't have to wonder for long. Stacked under his display counter, I saw a nest of porous crucibles and lids, the kind he'd use to make his brass.

Aside from the din of the Forum and the occasional blares and shrieks that rose above it, a stony silence threatened to settle around us until a gangling, copper-skinned youth arrived with Eran's order and laid the refreshments out on a worn but starched linen square that he draped over the display counter. Eran finished setting the table with a pair of tarnished silver goblets, their bases shaped like the talons of a raptor, and poured the water.

"Well, I can certainly see why your work is admired," I said as we took our places across from each other's frozen smiles. I couldn't say much more with a straight face. His creations were just too graceless, too flamboyant and ostentatious for my taste. So I slid my eyes down to my primly folded hands and studied the veins that meandered across their backs.

"Please, my dear, you must eat something."

I felt his chilly, viper-like eyes lock onto me, so I took a genteel bite of cheese. Thankfully, my hands did not shake, but an icy bead of sweat drilled down my back. When I caught his stare, he turned away, but his shoulders stiffened, and I wondered whether the stain on his forehead was darkening too.

We sat there blinking at each other.

He released a shallow breath.

I choked on my water.

His eyelid twitched.

I tried to keep a placid expression on my face.

His lips moved, but no words came out.

I forced open my own mouth to say something pleasantly irrelevant, but a lie tumbled out instead.

"Did Judah tell you I'll be leaving for Jerusalem soon?"

Surely that news would soften his defenses. Of course, I had no intention of going anywhere, not until I found out what I needed to know. And that glimpse of Drakon only rekindled my hope.

Eran cleared his throat.

"But you just got here. How unfortunate." He closed his eyes and waggled his head as if I'd brought news of a terrible tragedy and then pitched his gaze beyond my left shoulder. "Before you go, I insist you join Judah and me tomorrow. In gratitude for my having made the medallions, Alexander has invited me and my guests to attend first his reception in the Upper Palace and then the games in the stadium, where we'll sit with him in the *tribunal*. We could make it our little farewell party, you and I, my chance to show you the best Caesarea has to offer."

"How very thoughtful of you."

But even to my own ears, my tone sounded theatrical. Party? In truth, I was appalled at the prospect of witnessing another display of Roman bestiality. But Judah had asked me to meet Eran halfway. So going seemed the least I could do.

And why not one more lie?

"I am intrigued by your candlesticks, one in particular, the brass one over there." I pointed to a small but particularly gaudy one in the corner. "It would so grace my father's desk. Please, let me buy it from you."

"No, my dear, you must take it as a souvenir." His voice flowed like honey.

"Well then, at least let me contribute in your honor to the displaced peasants."

Taking his silence for consent as he wrapped the candlestick in a linen sheath, I left a few Tyrian shekels on his display counter. Stretching our lips into one more silky smile, our conversation ended with a series of deferential farewells punctuated by *tut*s and *tsk*s about the lack of rain or maybe the indolence of today's youth.

I remember my sense of relief as I opened the door. With the light streaming in, I looked back to wave a final goodbye, but Eran had already retreated to the bowels of his shop. Instead, I saw a few roaches scuttling around the statues. Feeling weightless, I flew into the sudden brilliance, the heat swishing over my body as I raced on anxious legs to hear what Phoebe had to report.

Chapter 18

Late Sunday Afternoon

"PHOEBE, I'VE BEEN going crazy. Where on earth have you been? You promised you'd come back to the inn right away." My voice split the air like a lash.

I'd been either pacing the floorboards while pounding my thighs with my fists or hinged forward on the edge of my cot, my head in my hands, conjuring up images of every disaster that could have befallen her. When I'd peek through the shutters to watch the shadows inch across the *cardo*, my eyes would pierce through every funnel of dust for some sign of her while the stench from the stables accompanied me like a bad dream. And all the while as I bit my lips, I'd taste my own blood, warm and salty.

"I did come back right away, and that right away is now," she said in her own prickly tone, standing before me, straight as a pole, arms crossed, her indignant chin pointing skyward. But then her poise withered, her shoulders slumped, her chin dropped, and the satchel fell to the floor with a clunk. Wiggling out of my himation and collapsing onto her cot, she lifted her head momentarily to mutter through pouting lips, "I thought you'd be proud of me."

Her disappointment hung in the air like a storm cloud.

Only then did I notice her clothes were coated with dust, her face flecked with dirt, and her bangs plastered to her forehead like a row of spikes.

"My precious Phoebe, I'm not only proud, I'm grateful, but I was worried just the same."

The tension in her face eased.

While crossing to the wash basin for a towel to wipe her face—I ended up having to call for the *puer* to bring us more—I tripped on the strap of the satchel.

"My goodness, what do you have in that satchel? Bricks?"

"You're close," she replied, rolling over and sitting up before leaning back on her elbows. "If Drakon noticed me, I wanted to look like I'd been shopping. So every once in a while, I'd pick up some stones to fill out the satchel. Besides, I thought hurling it could be a good diversion if I had to make a quick getaway. I tried to do exactly what you'd do. I even bought us some food on the way home, some cheese pastries at a *kapēleion*, but then I ate them myself. No sense going hungry just because I was on a dangerous mission."

"Well," I said with an indulgent smile, "I'm relieved to know you had lunch." And, in our embrace, I also caught the scent of honeyed pistachio nuts. "So tell me what you found out."

Her eyes brightened, and angling toward me as I perched on the crate near the foot of her cot, she began in a conspiratorial voice.

"I picked up his trail across from the textile shop. As slick as he is, he was still easy to track, at least at the beginning. I just had to follow his floating cloak. I know what I promised, Miriam, but before I knew it, he was darting across the Forum, passing between the marble lions that guard its north side, and exiting onto the *decumanus*. So I had to keep going, either that or scrub the mission, and then you wouldn't have the chance to hear my news."

Nodding with satisfaction, she got comfortable for the rest of her story, wriggling down to the foot of her cot, sitting on its edge, and smoothing her tunic over her knees. I knew then that she was going to keep me in suspense for every telling detail.

"Wait till you hear this," she said, leaning over to stab my shoulder with her index finger. "He turned west and headed directly to the Public Records Office. I figured if they have the same system here that we have in Alexandria, where you can pay a fee to secure a personal document, then he must be going there to retrieve a scroll. And sure enough, I was right."

"Well, did he get the recip—?" I asked, leaning forward, turning out my palms.

But she waved away my question as if she were brushing away a fly.

"See," she continued, "at first I didn't know what to do. Should I go in and risk his noticing me, or should I back into the shadow of the Forum's colonnade and risk compromising the mission? But knowing you, that you'd rather die than give up, I followed him inside."

I took a hard swallow.

"I wove my way through a clot of priests and businessmen, civil servants, scribes, and money changers, all thronging to enter its ornamental gate. Borne up the shallow flight of marble steps by the surge, I elbowed my way through the wide Corinthian-columned portico and the immense bronze-paneled double doors. Disheveled but otherwise intact, I entered the cavernous hall, only to be deafened by the chatter of official business reverberating against its canyon-like walls and blinded by the midday sun pouring its liquid spangles through the arched clerestory windows.

"One spangle must have caught Drakon's cloak because as soon as I straightened my tunic and adjusted your himation across my face, I spotted him in line at a service window. Falling in behind him so I could eavesdrop, I nevertheless kept my back turned and my head down while pretending to search through the satchel for the nonexistent token to claim some nonexistent document."

"Oh, Phoebe, you shouldn't have stood so close to him. That was much too dangerous." But I was too giddy to scold her.

"I wasn't afraid. I was too focused on what Drakon was doing to think about myself. But afterward, I felt a hammering in my chest.

"Anyway, he dug out of his purse a potsherd scratched with a list of items and a square lead token as thick as a coin with the numeral for box XIV embossed on both sides. He handed them to the next clerk, who by the way was missing an ear. Well, in almost no time, the clerk unlocked the wrought iron grille, stepped into the vault, and returned with five scrolls and a tablet. Drakon marked something on the tablet. I couldn't see what he was writing, so I let my eyes drift into the vault, you know, as if I had nothing on my mind and was just passing the time—its walls were lined with mahogany cabinets, each with scores of drawers—and then Drakon returned the tablet to the clerk, slipped the token back into his purse, and gathered up the scrolls. When he stepped aside to pack them into his satchel, I could feel a chill in the air he left behind."

Right then, I felt that same chill spasming through my own body.

"Slipping the satchel under his cloak and then slinging its strap diagonally across his body, he braced it against his hip with his forearm and then cruised through the blur. When I blinked again, he was standing under the portico, swiveling his head like a bird of prey before plunging into the swelter of the street. I could follow him only with my eyes as he strutted toward the harbor and turned south."

I heard footfalls at our door.

"Madame?"

I started when I heard a man's voice, but it was only the *puer*. Still, Phoebe and I froze like statues until he set down the towels and left. I was tempted to peek beyond the door to make sure he was gone, but remembering Judah's charge that I'd become obsessed, I squelched the urge and just stared at the door until I heard his footfalls on the stairs. Then I nodded for Phoebe to continue.

"Where was I?"

"Drakon left the Public Records Office."

"Oh, yes. Eventually I caught up with him but only by accident. By the time I wriggled my way to the street, he'd vanished as artfully as the man who killed that poor woman in the Forum. Still, I saw him head south, so that's the way I went.

"A briny breeze greeted me as I turned the corner, and the harbor unfurled before me. Sidling along the curve of the promenade, cutting through a stream of sun-browned stevedores and skirting the droves of tourists and rowdy sailors that clogged the walkway, I ducked and hid among the *horrea* whenever I saw a cloak floating in the breeze. Or I'd stand in the shade of one of those reception tents for tourists and calm my nerves with a few gulps of salty air."

"Oh, my poor Phoebe. I should never have let you talk me into this."

"But I haven't even gotten to the good part yet! You see, in the crush of the wharf, I'd all but given up hope of finding him. I was about to circle back to the inn when, upon nearing the land quay, I looked up at the Temple of Augustus and Roma and spotted someone sprinting up the stairway to its shelf above the harbor. Really, all I saw was a briskly-moving figure until Isis fanned a breeze to inflate his cloak and dispatched a sunbeam to catch its edge. Only then did I recognize the figure as Drakon. So, with the assurance of Isis's patronage, I inhaled a pocket of courage, ready to see what he was up to.

"I pounded up the Temple stairway, mounting the eastern of its two narrow flights of steps before ascending the expansive upper one, Isis propelling me now with a stiffer breeze, using her magic to empower me just as she'd used it to resurrect her brother-husband Osiris. I tore past the formal gardens, riding the fragrance of a hundred roses, and dashed through the antae, my heels whispering across the cool tessellated floor of the pronaos, my gaze halting momentarily on its coffered ceiling.

"And then my feet stuck to the floor. I heard the echo of two voices, one effete and uninflected, which I recognized as Drakon's, and the other guttural and ragged, its consonants hammering like a chisel against stone. Its timbre was so ear-scraping I pictured the statues of Augustus and Roma, as colossal as they are, cracking, toppling over, and tumbling into the sea.

"Venturing a peek into the naos, I saw Drakon shaking hands with a swarthy Parthian merchant swagged in fat. Apparently they'd already concluded their business because now the merchant was carrying the satchel, and Drakon was fingering a heavy purse that hung from his girdle.

"Still in the pronaos but trying to disappear, I flattened my buttocks against the back of the naos's rear wall, my ears ever alert to the two side exits as well as the front, more interested at that point in following the merchant since he had the scrolls. I heard a clip of footfalls hurrying toward the main portico—I figured they must be Drakon's—and immediately thereafter, the heavy slap of the merchant's *calcei* leaving through the northeastern portico and waddling down the steps onto the *Decumanus Maximus*.

"Then came the easy part: following the merchant. He didn't know me, hadn't seen me, and wouldn't recognize me. To him, I was just another faceless servant who hid in the skimpy shadows like everyone else that time of day. Little did he know I was on a covert mission to track a secret that could rock the Empire. But I kept the stones in my satchel and your himation across my face just the same on the off chance I might run into Drakon again, most unlikely with Isis protecting me, or equally unlikely, that I'd cross paths with the Parthian merchant in the future.

"I didn't have to follow him far before he entered Vesta's Teahouse, really just a graffiti-scarred courtyard with a cracked mud-brick floor, scattered containers of withered pomegranate trees, and a tattered canopy. Maybe you've noticed it, with its back to the Forum diagonally across from Eran's shop—"

"—That may have been the shop that catered the refreshments Eran ordered for me from an errand boy."

"So you know the place. Well, the merchant joined four oily men, hairy and dark, at a table behind a tightly woven wicker screen. At first they all looked alike, thick-faced and muddy-eyed, sprawled in their chairs, but then I saw differences among them. One in particular had a walleye that blinked constantly, and another had a rubbery face perched on a ringed neck as long as a pipe. The long-necked one—you'd have called him the Giraffe—would repeatedly clap Walleye on the back before melting into an explosive guffaw.

"Needless to say, I sat at the table immediately opposite the screen. My nose had to suffer their unwashed bodies, but I could stare directly at their table and catch their words before they floated away. Their language was foreign to my ears—the vowels flat, the consonants sharp—but their transaction was simple enough. The merchant took charge immediately, collecting his due in silver before distributing the scrolls in turn like a mother bird feeding her chicks. And then, as if on cue, all five heaved to their feet and shambled through the gate to fan out in all directions."

A musical sigh rolled out of Phoebe's mouth.

"So, that's my news, Miriam. Now tell me what it means."

"It means Saul and Judah's recipe is spreading through the Empire like fire through a hay stack, and it's all my fault. But it also means you're an intrepid assistant and a loyal scout. So let's celebrate your success tonight in the eatery of your choice."

Before the axe falls tomorrow.

Chapter 19

Early Monday Afternoon

THIS TIME PHOEBE let me wear the crimson, short-sleeved, ankle-length tunic. Humming merrily, she slipped it over my white, floor-length *tunica interior*, the one with the gold *instita*, and tied an embroidered sash firmly around my waist. But before declaring the ensemble suitable for the procurator's reception, she checked that the *instita* hung just below the hemline of my tunic.

"You need to flaunt your layers, Miriam. The more the better," she said as if I needed instruction on the rules of Roman fashion.

Next she plaited my hair and arranged the braids in a crown that she once again fixed in place with gold pins and dressed with the gold-threaded net. But when she brought out the *calamistrum*, I balked. We were already stifling in that airless cage of ours, thick with shadows even in the early afternoon, and choking on the stench from the stable yard. So she relented but only after a ragged breath and a theatrical sigh. Finally, she wrapped me in a freshly-fulled himation, fastened it at my shoulder with a fibula decorated with rubies, and pinned matching jewels to my ears.

"There!" she said, spinning me around and stepping back to admire the crimson waves swirling about my ankles.

Just then the *puer* knocked on our door to tell us the litter to carry me to the Upper Palace had arrived. As soon as I saw its polished fittings gleaming under the inn's rippling flag, its elaborately festooned gold drapes tied back to its fluted posts, and its slightly-parted white sheers fluttering in the warm breeze, I recalled the one other time I'd been carried so elegantly. Two years ago, Binyamin and I took a final spin around Alexandria before he was to depart for Rome en route to Capua. I pretended then we were on a celebratory excursion rather than in the closing chapter of our shared history. And I fixed on pretending this time that I'd be rushing to a reception in honor of my betrothal to Judah rather than to a display of Roman profligacy and barbarity.

Two *pedisequi* and four bearers attended the litter. Their well-oiled caramel bodies were dressed in the palest blue Indian cotton tunics trimmed with a row of silver buttons across each shoulder. And their feet were clad in deerskin *calcei*, the many straps fastened with silver buckles that made a line of glitter up their powerful calves.

They led me through a veil of heat into a cabin redolent of roses, banked with brightly-colored, overstuffed cushions, and paneled with scenes of Odysseus when, on a makeshift raft, he was swept back through the Strait of Messina to face Charybdis. Settling in, I closed the sheers to filter the light, and then before I knew it, I was gliding through the aether. Eddies of freedmen, slaves, and idlers stopped to gape as the bearers loped south along the *cardo* toward the two-tiered palace.

Hector had taught me all about Caesarea's two-tiered palace. Herod the Great built the Lower Palace on a promontory jutting into the Mediterranean so that it would occupy the entire peninsula and command a panoramic view of both the city and the sea. The Upper Palace, positioned above and along the eastern wall of the Lower Palace, was added later, at the same time as the stadium, to accommodate large-scale public receptions.

I'd just begun my betrothal fantasy when the litter swayed to a stop. The bearers, hardly panting from their climb, set me down in a park of topiaries clipped in the shapes of mythical animals. A nervous dampness swept across my chest then and still does whenever I recall standing on my stress-stiffened knees before the iron-slatted gateway guarded by a serried rank of soldiers. Their brass helmets crowned with a red crest and their sword belts hitched tight, their hobnail boots shifted on the crushed stone walkway as they held back the rearing mastiffs chained to their wrists.

When I turned to watch a gull spiral above the palace, I caught sight on my left of the broad, polished steps that descend to the Mediterranean and on my right, of the north end of the stadium. Then, turning again, my gaze reaching beyond the lip of the promontory, I saw unwinding before me images of the fili-greed coast and the fountains of seething foam that, silvered by the sun and whipped by the wind, relentlessly pound its glisten-ing rocks. These magnificent views may have primed me for the splendor of the Upper Palace's Peristyle Courtyard, but nothing could have prepared me for all that happened once I was inside the gate.

ERAN MET ME at the gate as soon as one of Alexander's freed-men announced my name. A servant then led us into a bustling anteroom, murals of the Battle of Actium decorating its soaring, gilt-edged walls and a geometric mosaic in onyx and sardonyx tessellating its polished floor. As soon as the servant took my himation, a steward led us to the immense Peristyle Courtyard, where guests were being greeted with a goblet of Faustian Falernian wine. Before taking a sip, they poured a few drops onto the floor as a libation to their gods. As the deltas of dark wine trickled between the tiles, I remembered the elderly Judean matron, a *sica* in her chest, her last drops of blood trickling between the cobbles that pave the Forum.

A white linen canopy suspended from the capitals of the courtyard's colonnade sheltered the hundreds of us from the harsh afternoon sun. At the same time, scores of Nubian houseboys waved palm fronds to augment the sea breeze and chase away the flies. Along the perimeter where many rooms open one to the other beneath the arcade, bouquets of roses bowed from their antique vases, censers smoldered with the fragrance of frankincense, and statues congregated in front of tapestries, their intricate designs depicting chariot races in the Circus Maximus, Roman soldiers wielding their swords, and the

Senate's deification of Julius Caesar.

My eyes ached as they scanned the men for Judah, but I saw only Roman faces, their skin fair, their heads rounded, their noses aquiline, and their hair layered in a futile attempt to conceal their bald spots. A few slouched on couches, but most stood in clusters along the colonnade droning in confident tones about business or politics. Some waggled their heads as they pursed their lips. Others whispered out of the side of their mouth as if they had the palsy. But all wore a toga of the finest white wool carefully draped in perfect folds, those in the elite classes flaunting a Tyrian purple stripe along its border. When their free arm emphasized a point of argument or beckoned to a crony, the stripe would lap at their noble red *calcei*.

I plunged into a throng of women jostling along a row of ornately carved screens toward the long tables of roasted meats that stretched like a belt across the width of the courtyard. They bobbed their heads like hens for a glimpse of the others' fashionably layered but by then rumpled skirts while clucking effusive greetings in perfect Latin.

Crushed against a rainbow of Chinese silks, I scrutinized their grooming while their skirts rustled the air, and their hems brushed the floor. Despite the reek of their cosmetics, which no amount of Arabian perfume could mask, their artful makeup amplified every feature and expression: their red ochre lips twitching into salon smiles, their lead paste foundation caking in the crease of every pucker, and their kohl-lined eyes darting flames of jealousy at the taller, blonder, and younger among them. To complete the spectacle, elaborate hairstyles accented with henna and threaded with jewels crowned their bobbing heads while the rest of their bodies bloomed with matching gemstones.

And then in the far corner I saw Judah. Wearing an indifferent expression and the green sleeveless tunic he had on when he met us at the harbor, he stood in the company of a short bronze statue and a tall, multi-wicked candelabrum. Flecks of sunlight edging the canopy dusted the contours of his body, his broad shoulders and their taper to a narrow waist. Seeing him stirred in me the same exquisite ache as when he walked me back to the inn from Eran's house, and I felt the pleasure of his body close to mine. But how was I going to steer my course through this thicket of finery? Best to inch along with the throng toward the refreshment tables, cross the courtyard there, and then carve my way along the less congested side.

Just then a hefty woman elbowed past me, slurring an "Excuse me." I was tempted to counter her jab with the left hook Binyamin had taught me, but instead I drew back to rub my sore rib. At that moment, a fleeting hush settled over the entire reception—even the canopy ceased snapping in the wind—and my ears fastened on a single phrase as it filtered through the screen:

"That dilapidated, excrement-encrusted synagogue they call a temple."

I just knew the voice referred to the little synagogue near my inn.

One furtive peek, and the image of two men poked through the scrollwork. Each wore a narrow stripe on his toga that identified him as an Equestrian, a member of the tiny elite class just below the rank of senator that manages the administrative and financial affairs of the Empire. They spoke too softly for me to catch more than a few snippets—the noise had begun to swell again—but one voice was laced with bitterness. The other, even more chilling, was cool and uninflected.

[A bark of laughter] "What can you expect from those stiff-necked Jews?"
[Inaudible]
"No! Not the gall to insult a Roman soldier! By Jupiter, they're more stubborn and pig-headed—"
[A long, malicious laugh that set off a dry, rasping cough]
"—than all the Greeks and Syrians put together."
[A few Latin words even Hector refused to teach me]
"—damn Jews in front of that synagogue. When the soldier passed, they turned their backs as one and

called out, 'Unclean! Unclean!' as if he were a leper."

"Alexander will make them pay. [Inaudible] too cocky. [Inaudible] crucify them."

"Never mind just them."

[A snicker of agreement]

"Yes, crucify the whole damn lot."

My blood froze. Frightful images of the pogrom flew before me like a kettle of vultures. I must have doubled over and slumped against one of the screens as the fear rattled through me because before I knew it, one of the stewards, probably thinking I'd had too much wine, was holding my elbow and escorting me to a chair under the arcade.

Eran raced to my side an instant later.

"My dear, are you ill? Your hands are trembling as if you caught a chill."

"No, it's just something I overheard."

When I repeated the essence of the conversation, Eran nodded knowingly.

"I've warned you, my dear, these are perilous times. Throughout Judea, our people are suffering. Our resistance, desperate now, is expressed in insults to their soldiers, but the hour is drawing near for the inevitable. As we speak, our soldiers, in caves and cellars, are preparing for a full-blown—"

His viper-like eyes flared with passion. Had he drunk too much wine? I became frightened for him. I was about to look for that telltale spittle at the corners of his mouth when we were interrupted.

"—Miriam bat Isaac, never did I expect to have the pleasure of seeing you again."

For an awkward moment, I couldn't place his name or his face. That's how disconcerted I was by Eran's warning. But as soon as I saw those impossibly long fingers, I recognized Gershon ben Israel, my companion on the *Orion* and Alexander's dealer in Faustian Falernian wine. Thankfully, I hadn't lost my wits altogether, so I could properly introduce Eran to him.

After the usual inquiries and pleasantries—yes, Eran knew

Gershon's host in Caesarea. They live in the same neighborhood; in fact Didius Bassus is his client—Eran said he was going to get Judah to stay with me until I'd fully recovered. And then he hurried off.

But Gershon stayed.

"Alexander extended me the invitation when he heard I was still in Caesarea." Gershon's voice was as mellow and as unhurried as ever. "And look who's here, someone else from Alexandria!" he said, his silver eyebrows bouncing with enthusiasm as he turned and extended his arm to gather in one of our long-lost countrymen. "Perhaps you remember him. If not, let me introduce Drakon, once the scribe to our dear friends, Amram ben Eleazar and his late son Noah, that is, before Fortuna brought him here to serve a grateful Alexander."

"Fancy meeting you here," he said, his tone saccharine but his jaw clenched.

I forced a smile, but my throat was suddenly too dry to speak.

Just then a freedman approached Gershon. "Mr. ben Israel, the procurator would like you to supervise the opening of another crate of your wine."

With that, Gershon excused himself, and any pretence of civility between Drakon and me left with him.

"Ben Israel might have been surprised to see me, but surely you're not, are you, Miss Snooty bat Isaac? I told you two years ago I'd been appointed to serve as the procurator's head scribe. And remember I said I'd use that opportunity to stir up trouble for you and your smarmy race? Well, the joke is on me. You and your people are doing a great job of that all by yourselves."

Prominent position or not, yellow spittle still flies out of his wicked mouth.

But he had more to say.

"Anyway, that's neither here nor there. After all, we go back a long way, don't we? Before that foul-smelling boyfriend of yours—may his soul be damned forever in the great pit of Tartarus—became the skimpy dinner for a squadron of blowflies. I'll bet he died of his own sickening breath, nothing compared to the stink of his putrefying body though. Well, at least he was relieved from having to marry you."

He vented more spleen with a sharp-edged cackle, but he still had one more insult to hurl. "Say, I hear you aspire to another boyfriend. Do you plan to steer him to an early grave too?"

The very shock of his words left me speechless, but he wasn't interested in a response anyway. Just like that encounter near Aspasia's, he ended his diatribe with a smirk and then turned on his heel and stalked away.

When I returned to my senses, I noticed Eran standing before me as if waiting for a reply.

"I'm sorry. Please ask me your question again."

"My dear, I haven't found Judah yet, but I wanted to get back to you as soon as that man left. I'm worried about leaving you alone. Your hands are still trembling. I was asking you whether you'd like me to bring you some food, perhaps something sweet like a dessert of frosted fruit. By the way, that man speaking to you? You looked like you knew him."

"Yes, his name is Drakon. I've known him for years. He used to work for my father's closest friend and business partner so he'd come to our house from time to—"

"*Shsh.* I think the procurator is about to address us."

As the noise ebbed, Alexander, flanked by his bodyguards, took his place along the northern colonnade and raised the imperial eagle atop his gilded staff. His eyes were watchful as they scanned the faces, but his expression was placid beneath a high fringe of dark curls that curved neatly over his polished stone brow. Waiting for the last murmurs to calm, he took a deep breath to summon up the power of his voice:

"I greet you in the name of Emperor Tiberius Claudius Caesar Augustus Germanicus."

His voice rang out over the courtyard with an elegance that belied his reputation for brutality. The crowd as one oozed toward him, his bodyguards raised their lances and standards, and the entire assembly roared, "Hail, Caesar!" I thought even the statues would salute him. As soon as the gathering quieted, I inched closer, so I could get more than a glimpse of this Roman

General and apostate from Judaism who orders the crucifixion of so many of our people.

Alexander was dressed in his military uniform, a breastplate of gold embedded with rubies, sapphires, and other gemstones worn over a silk, sleeveless tunic dyed imperial purple. He stood so still that even his heavily studded apron decorated with the tokens of his campaigns barely clinked as he spoke. He thanked us all for coming and made special mention of those who would be sitting with him in the *tribunal,* among them Eran ben Zahav for having crafted the winners' medallions and Gershon ben Israel for having brought his guests the most renowned wine in the Empire.

"So before following my ushers to the stadium, indulge once more in a goblet of this precious wine in honor of those who will be entertaining us with their lives. And long live the victors!"

Another roar from the crowd, and then a blur of skirts and belts, togas and tunics pressed past me toward the wine stewards while I stood in place, swiveling my head, wondering where on earth Judah was.

Chapter 20

Late Monday Afternoon

"WE WHO ARE about to die, salute you!" So proclaimed the gladiators as they stood in ranks before Alexander.

We guests of Alexander had missed the *pompa*, the garish early morning fanfare led by slaves in dazzling armor blowing their long, tinny trumpets. Right behind them in the death parade, we would have seen the gaudy floats with actors posing as mythological figures; musicians playing drums, horns, and flutes; and animal trainers showing off their beasts, the more exotic, the better. Then the excitement would have intensified as the other performers circled the arena: the hunters and bowmen, acrobats and dancers, jugglers and gymnasts, aerialists and wrestlers, and the *praegenarii*, those dwarfed, crippled, or deformed men who, using wooden weapons, mimic the gladiators to amuse the crowd.

Only then would the real gladiators have entered the arena through the *Porta Triumphalis*, the Gate of Triumph. As they brandished their weapons and flashed their shimmering cloaks to a thunderous ovation, the morning sunlight would have reached over the stadium's double eastern wall, stained their well-oiled bodies a bloody orange, and splashed their tangled shadows across the mica-flecked sand.

We'd missed the other preliminaries as well. But Alexander's privileged party would have been bored with them anyway, for only the serious business of torture, executions, and gladiatorial bouts, events scheduled nonstop from noon to sunset, could entertain such a world-weary coterie. Still, with the guests having lingered so long to indulge in Gershon's wine (while swaying like sailors to the rhythm of their own rustling garments, tinkling goblets, chatter, laughter, and sighs), we missed even the ever popular *damnatio ad bestia*, or condemnation to the beasts.

If there were no last minute changes in the program, then a slave from Gaul had been thrown to the lions for trying to run away. According to Hector, Augustus established this form of public execution after a Sicilian robber named Selerus had been pilloried on a high platform in the Forum. When the platform happened to collapse, he fell into a cage of wild beasts. The sight was so amusing to those who came to taunt him that *damnatio ad bestia* became a regular feature of the games. And once, when Caligula faced a shortage of condemned criminals, he ordered his soldiers to seize an entire section of spectators and have them thrown to the lions instead.

But Alexander's guests were most eager for the ultimate gladiatorial bout, the last event of the day, when a little-known but promising Agrippa Fortitudo would be pitted against the betting favorite and most popular gladiator in the Empire. Having survived five years in the arena, Orcus, with a victory tonight, would add freedom to his purse.

What a sight! Thousands filled the four tiers of the stadium. The rows of sandstone seats, freshly washed and smelling of lemon and thyme, wrapped around all but the west side so spectators, should they weary of the butchery, could stretch their eyes across the arena to a shimmering sea melting into the horizon. The first tier, closest to the floor of the arena and protected from the wild beast hunts by archers along a wooden balustrade, is reserved for senators, magistrates, other noble patricians, and priests, each distinguished by the stripe, border, or color of his toga. The rest of the spectators are likewise assigned to a tier according to their status: the second for Equestrians, those ranking just below the patricians; the third for wealthy plebeians; and the fourth for the ordinary plebeians and common women. Without the shade of the awning that slopes down from the top of the third tier, the folks in this highest tier bake under the brutal sun.

Eran, Gershon, Judah, and I, of course, sat in the spacious

tribunal, a magnificent balcony of ringside boxes in the most prominent position in the first tier, the middle of the south side of the arena. The procurator's *bisellium,* a wide, cushioned, ornate chair on which Alexander reclined in his purple robe and gilded wreath, occupies the center of the *tribunal.* Immediately behind him stood the sentries and a cohort of slaves swishing ornate fans, and behind them, a row of tall, intricately carved censers. I sat next to Eran, who took the seat on Alexander's right; then Gershon, on the procurator's left, and Judah next to him. So much the better. I didn't want to look at Judah anyway, let alone speak to him. He'd avoided me during the reception, and I didn't know why.

Not then.

Just as the usher seated us, the last of the *praegenarii* were engaged in a bloodless duel while crews of slaves in bright tunics prepared the rest of the arena for the standard gladiatorial bouts. Some raked fresh sand over the hunks of sinew, opalescent entrails, and splotches of blood left from the wild animal hunts. Others, to mask the sour smell of fear and the festering stench of death, heated cones from the aromatic pine trees planted around the stadium.

But nothing could fool the rats and the flies.

While the *praegenarii* clowned, spectators began summoning bookmakers and roving food vendors or sidling through the aisles to make their way under the stands, past the souvenir hawkers, to the snack bar and latrines. And then the trumpets blared, a fever of anticipation spread through the stadium, and two gladiators amid ecstatic applause entered the arena through the *Porta Triumphalis:* a *thraex* and a *murmillo,* each armed with a weapon, shield, and visored helmet. Whereas the husky *murmillo* would have to count on his muscular arms and upper body strength to wield his long sword and large rectangular shield, the *thraex,* taller, leaner, and protected by only a small, almost square shield, would have to rely on his quickness with a *sica* to slash or stab his opponent.

I vowed to watch, to look for some justification for this deadliest sport. I sat forward, my elbows on my knees, my chin on my folded hands, and my eyes fixed on the center of the arena, its pristine sand a lemon-tinted carpet in the afternoon light.

The bout began as a sparring match, the pair circling, measuring each other, their thick leather soles grating against the sand. They slashed the air with a few feinting blows while the fans held their breath, waiting for the first strike.

And then a whack; the *murmillo*'s sword struck his opponent's shield. Hard. The thud of metal against wood and the trill of the blade. The *thraex* staggered back, reaching out to clutch a tuft of air. Regaining his balance, he spun around. Then, in a blinding flash, he raised his *sica* and moved in fast with a series of furious jabs.

Too fast. A collective gasp tore through the stadium as a few fans dashed into the aisles to get a better view. The *murmillo* struck the side of his opponent's helmet with a barrage of blows, his beefy shoulders heaving with each jolt. Then his sword nicked the *thraex*'s defensive arm. An angry red ribbon spilled onto the sand. The fans sprang to their feet in a frenzy of bloodlust, waving their fists, bobbing their heads, chanting *"Hoc Habet!"* "Now he's had it!"

And indeed he had. His arm weakened; his shield fell away.

The *murmillo* closed in, kicked him in the groin. The *thraex* sailed through space, his limbs pinwheeling, time all but stopping until he hit the floor of the arena, the fans fiercely attentive until an audible splintering of bone released a savage chorus.

The *thraex*, thrashing like a fish on the beach, raised his left hand, his index finger extended, his request for mercy. The *murmillo* straddled him. All eyes shifted to Alexander. He surveyed the crowd with apparent gravity. All thumbs turned. He paused, a slight smirk creased the corners of his mouth, and then his own thumb turned.

Eran said the *thraex* deserved to die because he fought mechanically, without the Roman will to win.

And so, with another thunderous ovation, the *thraex* grasped the victor's thigh to signal he was ready to accept his opponent's sword through his neck. A thrust and a grunt from the *murmillo*; a shriek and a fountain of blood from the *thraex*.

Eran said the shriek only proved the *thraex* lacked the contempt for pain and death that the games are meant to glorify.

The once pristine sand had turned a slaughterous red. The ritual all but over, the spectators awaited only an attendant dressed as Charon, the bearded ferryman of Hades. Out he rushed, wearing a conical hat and red *exomis*, a short, left-sleeved tunic that bares the right half of his chest. Carrying his massive, emblematic hammer, he squatted from an isosceles stance and struck the forehead of the fallen gladiator.

Eran said too many gladiators have tried to feign their own death. So the blow is to forestall fakery and make sure he's really dead before the attendant drags him to the *spoliarium*, the pit below the arena where the bodies of the slain beasts and gladiators are dumped to await mass burial. But I've since heard that the bodies of the gladiators are fed to the wild animals to whet their appetite for human flesh.

Finally, amid hysterical applause, the *murmillo* approached the *tribunal*, his body drenched in blood, his face glistening with sweat. He saluted the procurator and bowed to all whereupon Alexander tossed him a gold medallion on a silk sash. He donned the medallion, bowed once more, and, stepping through the puddles of blood that stained the carpet of sand, he crossed the arena and disappeared through the *Portal Triumphalis*.

The stadium began to spin. A briny foam spewed up my gorge and soured my mouth. I swallowed the slime, grabbed my ankles, and dropped my head to my knees to calm the spasms.

"Are you all right, my dear?" At least Eran noticed my discomfort.

But I dared not raise my head. Instead, my arms dangling at my sides, I answered with a flap of my hands.

"Please, let me get you something to eat."

His voice sounded so far away.

Again I flapped my hands, this time waggling my head with a moan.

"Then let me take you back to the palace where you can lie down."

I dug my nails into my palms so I could find my tongue. "No, I'm sure it will pass. I just need a minute. I'll be fine." I was determined to show both Judah and Eran that I had the grit to see this day through.

When the spasms subsided, I pinched my cheeks, wiped my clammy hands on my tunic, and slowly raised my head.

To see another bout.

And another.

And then I lost count.

I looked up to see that the awning had been retracted, that the sinking afternoon sun, glowing scarlet by then, had tinted the sea a bloody red.

"My dear, are you sure I can't get you something?"

The chilly breath of a late-afternoon breeze sent a shiver up my spine. I wrapped my arms around my himation just as the last blare of the trumpets signaled the final bout, the one everybody had been waiting for. Orcus was only a few minutes away from freedom.

I remember Binyamin describing the contest between a *retiarius* and a *secutor* as his favorite. The *retiarius*, the only type of gladiator to fight without a helmet, uses just a trident and a circular net. Accordingly, the most handsome gladiators are assigned to train as a *retiarius* so by their looks alone, they can attract a following, especially among women. The *secutor* fights with a dagger, shield, and armor, but his helmet both protects him from and exposes him to the *retiarius's* net. Enclosing the *secutor's* entire head, the surface of the helmet is smooth so the net slides off easily, but its tiny eyeholes narrow his field of vision. So the *secutor* has to get well within the range of the net to attack his opponent. Others favor this pairing so that if the *secutor* is victorious, they can watch the *retiarius's* face when he confronts his own death.

A raucous crescendo welcomed the gladiators as they entered the arena. But amid the commotion, the cheering for Orcus and the jeering for his opponent, a violent shudder ripped through me.

"What is it, my dear? Are you feeling ill again?"

"Where is this troop from?"

"Why from Capua, the most famous *ludus* in the Empire."

Then I knew what my eyes had already told me, that the full lips and ginger curls, the flattened but still aggressive nose, and the left cheek with its threadlike scar belonged to Binyamin, my twin brother, the one who'd dreamed of becoming a warrior since our earliest excursions into the countryside when we'd glimpse the retired legionnaires' lavish estates. Later, when he learned their term of service was a long twenty-five years, he focused instead on becoming a gladiator. My brother held fast to that dream despite his shrill arguments with Papa, who warned him that he'd lose everything, not only his rights as a Roman citizen but the ownership of his very life.

Yes, Agrippa Fortitudo was my handsome brother, always the exceptional athlete, the formidable competitor with a noble physique, the risk-taker, the admirer of all that is Roman, who gave up his liberty and birthright for this chance to die with slaves, criminals, and prisoners of war for the amusement of a Roman mob.

He brandished his net as he darted in and out, evading the *secutor*'s dagger, poised to drive home his trident, casting his net, missing his target, pulling the cord to snatch it back, rushing in again, dragging rather than lifting his sandaled feet across the sand to maintain his traction, a technique he'd taught me years ago. But Orcus was cunning. He landed a hit with his dagger. Binyamin bled from the belly. I couldn't bear to see his blood.

But a *secutor* must win quickly. His helmet allows him little air, and he's encumbered by the weight of his shield and armor. Orcus may have been the favorite, but he'd never faced Binyamin, an impressive adversary even as a young ephebe, when he unintentionally killed the fair, husky Titus in their first competition in the Gymnasium's school for combative sports.

And so the bout was far from over, every passing minute to Binyamin's advantage. Round and round they went, the flight of the net, the thrust of the dagger.

The fans began to fidget. By now, their hero should have finished off the upstart and claimed his freedom. The daylight was draining into the shadows; the sun was collapsing into the sea. Once more the fans sprang to their feet, waving their fists, shouting *"Verbera!" "*Strike!"

I felt another caustic stream roll up my gorge. Despite the chill, I was bathed in sweat. I thought of dropping my head to my knees again, but my eyes stayed riveted on the arena. Another violent shudder, a gag, and a disabling fear engulfed me.

Once more the net flew. But this time, Orcus couldn't escape. His legs were ensnared in the net. Binyamin closed in with his trident. The stadium was suddenly, eerily silent; the fans, stunned. And this time Alexander didn't survey the crowd before turning his own thumb. Perhaps he wanted to see what this newcomer was made of, or perhaps he just wanted to watch the *retiarius*'s face when he plunged his trident into the beloved *secutor*'s chest.

But I couldn't watch. Instead, I leaped to my feet and dashed toward an exit, leading I knew not where. In my madness, I jumped over the balcony into a common passageway, already clotted with others seeking to exit before the rush. But I was lost, confused, so many people, their long shadows tumbling out of the tiers into the passageways. All I wanted was to find Binyamin. How could I get to him without crossing the arena? I had to see him, had to talk to him, before I left.

My legs racing against the dying light, I was propelled by a deeper darkness within me. I forgot for the moment where I was going, how long I'd been running, or why, but eventually I exhausted myself enough to stop and think. That's when I decided to backtrack, to look for the latrines and from there, for a tunnel that might lead still lower, to the *spoliarium* and the other chambers below the arena.

I turned abruptly to the right, and that's when I felt a blade slash me from behind.

Chapter 21

Monday Evening

THE DAGGER LODGED in that sliver of space below my left armpit and got caught in the underside of my sleeve. Its edge threatened to cut me, but I managed to grasp the handle and slide out the blade by raising my left arm and reaching across my chest, toward my back with my right. But by the time I removed it and turned around, no one was about other than the river of fans pouring out of the upper tiers.

The darkness had closed in too much for me to see more than the length and curve of the dagger, but it was a *sica* all right. That's when I smacked my forehead and took a step back. Of course! Phoebe had been right when she said the killer in the Forum had been aiming for me. And whoever he was, he hadn't given up. I was saved this time by my sudden turn to look for Binyamin just as I'd been saved then by the Judean matron scuttling in front of me when that monstrous dog attacked the cavalryman's horse.

The realization that I was responsible for the old woman's death hit me like a blow from Charon's hammer. Strangely enough though, the anguish soon gave way to both a savage thrill for having survived and a shame-filled relief that the tragedy befell her instead of me. And perhaps just as strange, when I tucked the *sica* inside the back of my sash, my thoughts pulsed with resolve rather than with the bowel-constricting fears that used to paralyze me. I'd already managed to find out that Drakon was the one making copies of the recipe and selling them to others including Eran, and with that same determination, I was going to find out why the *Sicarii* had targeted me for assassination.

At first I wondered whether the assaults were connected to my pursuit of the recipe. Unlikely, I figured, if Drakon was behind the assaults. The first attempt came before Drakon even knew I was in Caesarea. Besides, he surely couldn't be a member of the *Sicarii*. Okay, he could have adopted their modus operandi, but for what reason? He couldn't still be angry for my supposedly having gotten Noah to fire him. And the assassination of a Roman citizen carries the *summum supplicium*. How could any attempt on my life be worth that risk?

Next I hypothesized that the two assaults were independent events, that Phoebe was wrong and Eran was right, that a member of the *Sicarii*, though not necessarily the woman's husband, killed her intentionally. *But no*, I thought, waggling my head. *That I should twice have come so close to being killed in the same way, with a sica and in a crowd, is too much of a coincidence.*

Besides, Drakon could have known about my presence in Caesarea long before he saw me at today's reception. After all, he must have known Eran at least since early May, when Judah sent me the letter. Soon after my first Shabbat here, Eran could have told Drakon of my visit and in particular, of my interest in the recipe. In any case, if Drakon believed that Eran could have confided the source of his recipe to me, then he might be afraid that just for spite, I'd report him for dealing in subversive documents, yet another offense punishable by the *summum supplicium*.

Yes, the more I thought about it, the more convinced I became that Drakon could reasonably believe he had nothing to lose, nothing at—

And then a fear-clogged voice calling my name rolled over the stream of spectators.

I waited to hear it again, to see where it came from.

"Miriam! Where have you been? Eran and I have been looking all over for you. One minute you're in the *tribunal*, and the next minute you're gone."

I felt a childish triumph as I noted the creases in Judah's brow and the constriction of his voice.

"All of a sudden, I got so queasy from the glare, the monotony, the gales of hysteria, and the stench of violence that I had to find a latrine quickly. But don't worry about me," I added even though I knew the irony would be wasted on him. "Besides, I don't want to ride back in a litter. I need the fresh air. Just thank Eran for me."

And then as an afterthought, "By the way, where is he now?"

"He went off to search for you in the other direction."

"Everyone's been so kind." More wasted irony. "Well, tell him I'm much better, and I'll find my own way back to the inn."

But first, I've got to find Binyamin. I know he's here, and if I don't see him now, he could end up as food for the lions before I get another chance.

Chapter 22

Late Monday Evening into Monday Night

SLOGGING MY WAY against a tide of spectators, I hustled toward the latrines, hoping to find some sort of passageway but retching along the way from the stench. Once there, slipping and lurching in the runnels of overflowing sewage, I stretched my eyes into the darkness. That's when I saw a circle of light, small and dim, hollowing out a mound of earth that was the entrance to a tunnel.

As I descended through the narrow passageway, torches stared out at me and splayed my furry shadow against the soot-streaked walls. The insufferable reek of rotting flesh, so unbearably sweet, crowded the air and settled on my lips while a pulsating heat rushed out to parch my skin. Able at last to see for some distance into this netherworld and feeling the slope of the tunnel leveling off, I figured I was approaching the *hypogeum*, the vast network of cells and chambers beneath the arena.

At first the hairs at the nape of my neck would prickle whenever a soldier snared me with his gaze and darted a flame of suspicion at me. All were hulking brutes with leathery faces and hands the size of shovels. Some stood guard like fence posts. Others tromped through the passageways, their heavy boots beating a steady rhythm of thuds against the hard stones as they hastened to carry out the orders spooling out of the chief officer's quarters. One by one they'd appraise me with their needle eyes, only to dismiss me with the trace of a smirk as nothing more than a bedraggled whore sent to entertain the victors. So soon enough I realized I could wander through the tunnel and its branches with impunity.

The labyrinth reminded me of the crypts and corridors beneath the Serapeum, which I toured as a young girl with Phoebe, Aunt Hannah, and our much loved slave and second mother, Iphigenia. We too had smelled the fear of the sacrificial animals and saw in each chamber the smudged faces and white eyes of those fated to work there. But at least an ancient coolness breathed out of the bare stone walls. And my nose rewarded me with the pleasures of frankincense, myrrh, and nard in the incense laboratories and cardamom, honey, and cassia in the bakeries.

Well into the *hypogeum* by then, passing its lurid pockets of light, I dared to look through tightly barred grilles into the cages of the hundreds of beasts doomed to die: lions, tigers, and bears but also crocodiles, apes, zebras, ostriches, and hyenas, animals varied and novel enough to demonstrate the vastness and power of the Empire. In other chambers, I saw the winches, capstans, ropes, and pulleys the stage mechanics use to hoist the animals into the arena. Once, when the equipment failed, Claudius ordered those responsible for the malfunction to fight in the animals' places.

More bleak passageways, grim chambers, and grisly cells. Many I couldn't see into. So swallowed by shadows, they emitted only the stench and groans of human misery or the clamor of slaves sharpening swords, hammering out armor, or testing whips. But I could identify the *spoliarium* because in addition to the stench of slaughter, the squeals of rats, and the din of slaves stripping armor and weaponry from the dead, I could see in a puddle of light the rows upon rows of stacked corpses yet to be stripped.

Binyamin, however, being an *auctoratus* or hired gladiator, would be too valuable a property, even if mortally wounded, to be struck with "Charon's" hammer and dumped in the *spoliarium*. He'd be carried out of the arena with dignity, borne on a stretcher rather than dragged by his heels, and brought to the *saniarium* to be treated. So that was the chamber I had to search for.

And so I continued, pulled through the shadows by that inviolable bond to my own flesh and blood, past cell after cell of the condemned stinking in their filth, crying out to their gods. Their strangled sobs and wails of misery would ring along the walls until, as my heels clicked on, their laments were replaced by a fresh chorus of agony. Sometimes I'd backtrack to probe a tunnel I thought I might have missed. I could never be sure. All the walls reeked of despair, and all the cells printed the same macabre afterimage on the screen inside my eyelids.

And then, in another tunnel, some salutary signs reached out to me: the odors of opium and astringents; of mossy herbs wrapped in linen; and of salves blended from ibis fat, honey, and lint. Along with these, I heard the whistles and wheezes of men thick with sleep, their phlegmy snores fed by eddies of smoke from censers burning mandrake root. And from around the corner, I listened to the banter of cronies: their rollicking guffaws and gusty backslaps, their Vulgar Latin spiked with lewd slang, and their wine-logged voices exchanging ribald jests and bawdy anecdotes.

That's when I recognized a familiar voice, common like the others but with softer consonants.

I didn't rush to the grille, grab the bars, and call breathlessly to my brother as I imagined I would. Instead, controlling that impulse, I smoothed down my hair, adjusted the folds of my himation, dusted the soil from my clothes, scraped the mire from the soles of my sandals, and pressed my back against the adjacent wall as if by doing so I could disappear into its stones. Then I turned my head, tipped it sideways ever so slightly, and sent a long glance into the cell through the corners of my eyes so I could take measure of him unseen.

My gaze first brushed the grime-stained walls of his cell, each lit by a torch that hurled up a ragged flame and a ribbon of dirty orange smoke. Next it flitted to the single oil lamp suspended from the center of the ceiling. Its amber light fanned out over a cot draped in spotless linen and a squat table jammed with vials of herbs, alabastra of unguents, flasks of vinegar, amphorae of wine, towers of bandages, and trays of syringes. Finally my eyes settled on the man lying there, naked but for the tattoos on his face, legs, and hands and the medallion around his neck.

Face up, leaning back on the pillows that elevated his upper body, his arms raised and bent like wings, he cradled his head in his laced hands. His trainers, while keeping up their toadying blather, snaked over him, massaging his skin with unguents, applying poultices to the bruises blooming on his chest, stanching the flow of blood from the cuts on his face, and cleaning the gash in his belly that oozed a putrid cream.

I waited for a break in their badinage before I let out a full breath. Then I pinched my cheeks, squared my shoulders, and ventured toward the grille.

After a long moment, my brother rubbed his eyes with the heels of his palms. "Hey, Sis, is that really you or"—turning to his trainers—"did you guys put too much opium in my wine?"

He leaned forward, staring through the grille in disbelief. "How did you get in here?" His voice was low, his diction only slightly slurred. Waggling his head in wonderment, he added by way of an explanation, "Well, you are my sister after all, my twin at that. I hope you didn't have to fight your way in here, but I like to think you remember the moves I taught you."

Then, after a bark of laughter and hardly a pause, he began speaking again, this time rapidly, as if under the spell of too much yellow bile, his eyes dilated with excitement, his voice ripping through the tunnel. "Did you see the bout, Sis? What did you think of your brother and his Roman courage then? How did you like the way I killed Orcus? One plunge through his chest, and he was a goner. I tell you the fame of Agrippa Fortitudo was made tonight. Starting tomorrow, women will be lined up to moon over me, that's for sure. Just like Zenon's daughter, that tart who'd relieve my lust in the pantry of her father's cookshop. Remember that, Sis, when Papa used to ground me, and I'd jump out my window and hang out there?"

Other memories hummed through my head instead, like when we'd go swimming, and Binyamin would slice through the waves as gracefully as any fish or when we'd set out for the harbor, and he'd vault onto the back of a mule cart to hitch a ride. In keeping with that shared childhood and to have a private word with him, I switched from Latin to our Alexandrian Greek.

"Binny, Binny, you could have been killed tonight! Listen, I want you to come home with me. I can sell my share of our mother's jewelry and buy out your contract. Please, Binny."

He faced me four square. An unexpected silence grew between us, and then his eyes slid away. Sitting up still more, he winced in pain before vomiting up a fountain of glutinous chunks and spewing them into the chamber pot alongside his cot. After that, his lips froze in a manic grin. I thought he might be considering my offer. But no. He must have been trying instead to control the spasms because a minute later, he was throwing back his head and dismissing the plan with a whoop of laughter and a sweep of his hand.

I could see that his face, though still handsome, had lost its youthful appeal. It had gotten fuller, even bloated, and accumulated a constellation of fresh scars. Yes, he was still magnetic, his body more powerful than ever, but if I'd had to pick him out on the street, I might have passed him by as just another Roman thug.

"Look, Sis, if you came all this way to drag me home like a sniveling weakling, you've wasted your time. I'll never give up being a gladiator until I'm awarded the *primus palus* or killed in the attempt, and I'll never go back to Alexandria even for a visit as long as Papa is alive. You should know better than that."

He spoke the words gently, but the earth sank beneath my feet.

And I felt my shoulders droop.

Yes, I should have known better. But he is my brother, though I could easily lose my certainty about even that. Like Tiberius Julius Alexander, he's forsaken our heritage. He violates our dietary laws, profanes our Shabbat, and engages in careless sex with wanton women, all forbidden by the Torah.

He's a Roman now, no longer a Jew.

I could have stood before him bleeding tears, but it was too late for that. So, with a mumble of clichés, I turned to leave.

"Wait, Sis."

Had he changed his mind?

But no. I was wrong again.

"Let Albus show you out. My gapped-toothed friend here knows this maze better than anyone."

Binyamin called to him in Latin. Albus stopped massaging Binyamin's legs, wiped his hands on his tunic, took the key that dangled from his belt, unlocked the grille, and then locked it again from the outside.

As he mutely led me through the tunnels, I could feel the air growing cooler as we approached the entrance. From there I easily found my way past the latrines, around a thicket, and through some hedges to the *cardo*. The city was well lit by a white moon and the fire atop the Drusion. And so, despite the sting of tears, I plucked at my skirts to raise the hem and ran back to the inn as if by doing so I could escape the anguish in my heart.

Chapter 23

Tuesday Morning

SNEAKING A FEW peeks through the fringe of my eyelashes while pretending to be asleep, I caught glimpses of Phoebe getting up and preparing to go to the Forum to replenish our supply of toiletries. And so I was able, temporarily at least, to escape her questions about the reception, the games, and most of all about the slash in my himation and the cut in the sleeve of my tunic. Assuming she'd stop in to visit Bion, I figured I had the rest of the morning here in the *cella* to pursue my own questions like who was trying to kill me and why. So far my best clue was the *sica* itself, which I'd wrapped in yesterday's finery, soiled and torn beyond repair, and stuffed into the rattan chest while Phoebe remained blissfully asleep, her lips parted in a tender half-smile.

She'd stirred last night when I lit the candelabrum by my cot—she'd rolled onto her back, heaved a sigh, and then turned onto her other side—but she quickly spiraled back into slow, rhythmic breaths. As for me, fearful of the nightmares the evening's events might conjure up, I hardly closed my eyes. Nonetheless, as I tossed in that wilderness between sleep and wakefulness, a senseless pattern of chilling images haunted me: of Charon raising his massive hammer to strike Binyamin's forehead while he lay inert on the arena floor; of Binyamin in his cell, his face turning blue as he choked on his own fluids; and of a shapeless assassin with luminous gray fangs chasing me. These grotesque fantasies unnerved me so that I rose with a sour stomach and found myself groping for my vial of *acidum salis* before remembering I'd stuffed it into the chest along with the *sica*.

I stumbled out of bed and stood with the aches of a body bowed with age. Nevertheless, as soon as my feet touched the splintery floorboards, I shuffled over to the chest to get the vial and make sure the *sica* was still there. Relief washed over me when I felt it inside its cocoon. My memory of stashing it last night was real, not just another figment of my grotesque imaginings.

I unwrapped the *sica*, brought it with the vial to the table, and folded back the shutters to coax in what little light there was. But one gamey whiff of the stable yard was enough for my rebellious stomach. So back to the chest I went to get a candle and that gaudy little candlestick from Eran, still encased in its linen sheath. As soon as I planted the candle in the cup and got a flame to leap out of the wick, I closed the shutters and looked at the *sica*.

That's when I got my first surprise of the morning. Even before examining it closely, I could see the emblem on its handle, a crude outline of a radiant sun, the very same emblem on both Eran's seal ring and the *sica* that killed the Judean matron. The match only confirmed my conviction that the old woman had been killed in my place. But why did Eran, a friend to the most powerful Roman in Judea and someone the *Sicarii* would call a Greek Jew, have that same emblem? Was he keeping the seal ring as evidence against someone in the *Sicarii*, or was he himself mixed up with them? And why were the *Sicarii* after me? As far as I knew, no one else I'd been with during my first few days here had been threatened, not even Gershon or Eran, who'd appear more likely than I to be collaborating with Rome. No, it didn't make sense. I was missing something.

Then I heard a tiptoe up the stairs and saw a shadow under the door sliding toward me. As the door creaked open, the candle flame rippled in the draft. I picked up the *sica* in my right hand, hid it behind my back, and readied myself for action, my left leg in front, pointing forward, its knee poised to lunge, my hips squared, and my weight balanced on the right foot, toes spread, thigh firm, just as Binyamin taught me when we'd play soldiers.

I took a deep breath, held my position, and watched a head curl around the half-open door and poke inside.

Perhaps we both shrieked, but after that, I heard only the intruder sting me with a rebuke.

"Miriam, why are you standing there like a statue? And as long as you're up, why are you still in your *capitium*? Half the day is gone."

"Oh, Phoebe, you scared me. I didn't expect you back so soon. I thought you'd stop in to see Bion."

"I'll see him later. I wanted to come back here first to put away the toiletries and see how you were, but I didn't want to disturb you in case you were still sleeping. I meant to stay up last night so I could hear all about your day, but before I knew it, my eyes were full of sand. Besides, I knew no matter how late the hour, Judah would see you back here safely. So I went to bed.

"Now tell me. Were you pleased with how you looked? How was the food? Did you sit next to Judah at the games? Did Eran introduce you to the procurator? Did you see any other famous . . ."

While the head of one question chased the tail of the next, my right arm relaxed.

"Miriam," Phoebe said with a gasp, "what are you doing with that dagger in your hand? You look like you're ready to kill—"

And then some horror must have gripped her because her jaw dropped and stiffened in that position. The room filled with silence while, in the trembling light of that one candle, I watched her lips struggle to form words. We stood there frozen, our eyes locked, until she was able to close her mouth, swallow, and regain power over her tongue.

"I think you'd better tell me what's going on." Her voice was barely audible.

While trying to craft some semblance of an explanation— she worries so much that I never know how much of the truth to tell her—I turned around to lay the *sica* on the table. But I was so engrossed in concocting a credible story that I knocked over the vial of *acidum salis*, breaking the neck of the vessel and causing some of it to splash onto the blade of the *sica* and the base of the candlestick.

Phoebe would later claim Isis had loosened my grip.

"Now look what a mess I've made. Quick, Phoebe, a towel!"

And that's when I got my second surprise of the morning.

"Phoebe, never mind the towel. Just come quickly. Look what's happening."

She dropped the satchel of toiletries and rushed to my side. Bowing over the table, her head swiveling back and forth, she peered at the puddles with a puzzled brow. "I don't understand, Miriam. What am I supposed to see?"

"First compare the dagger and the candlestick. They're the same golden color, an amazing coincidence since this shade of brass is so unusual. And by the way, I happen to know that Eran compounded the brass for the candlestick.

"And look, a fizz is bubbling on both and leaving a fine, white powdery residue. No surprise there, I guess. *Acidum salis* reacts with brass."

"So what does that mean?"

"I'm not sure yet. Please, I'll need that towel after all."

I used the towel to dry a shard from the neck of the vial. Holding the shard by its edge, I dipped a corner into a puddle of the *acidum salis* and let a few drops dribble first onto the dagger and then onto the candlestick. Then I did it again. And again.

"What is it, Miriam? What do you see?"

"The bubbles foaming on the dagger and candlestick are the same size and color, and they're forming at the same rate. And look, a white powder is also forming on both."

"I still don't get it."

But I did. With this more precise evidence, I knew with certainty that the brass in the *sica* had the same proportion of calamine as the brass in the candlestick. In short, Eran must have compounded both samples of brass and had probably cast both pieces as well.

"It means, Phoebe, that Eran made this dagger. It was used in an attempt to kill me last night."

"Miriam, I think you'd better start from the beginning."

Chapter 24

Tuesday Early Afternoon

I TOLD PHOEBE the whole story except the part about my recognizing Binyamin in the arena and visiting him in the *hypogeum*. I was too ashamed to acknowledge even to her that my brother had not only joined the dregs of humanity but had become one himself.

She listened calmly with few interruptions until I got to the assault.

"Is that what you call this thing, a *sica?*" she asked, her child-like features tightening into a grimace as she balanced it across her trembling palms. "Because of its curve?"

I was about to show her the torn clothes, how the *sica* had cut through my himation but missed my flesh, when the *puer* knocked and announced through the door that some man named Judah was waiting in the dining room to see me.

"I knew it. He's come to apologize for his inattentiveness. After all, you went to the reception and games for his sake."

"But Phoebe, I'm not ready! Please tell him I'll be a while, and then come back and help me dress."

In the meantime, I washed and dried the *sica* and candlestick, rolled each in a towel, and packed them into the satchel to bring downstairs.

I PASSED THROUGH the clouds of cheap frying oil and flatulence that hung over the foyer and regarded Judah for a moment before entering the near-empty dining room. He sat facing me from a table in the far corner. The dirty dishes on the sideboard, with their skins of grease, dregs of soup, and clots of gravy, made me wonder whether the inn sold its luncheon scraps as swill to the stable yard next door.

A few slivers of afternoon sunlight wriggled through the dusty shutters to print furry stripes across the tables. Others stretched across the room to highlight the smudges on the murals, the tatters on the cushions, the tarnish on the fixtures, and the chinks in the crystal before scattering their last glimmer across the floor's grime-streaked Olympians. Judah was leaning forward, talking to the air like an actor in rehearsal, but given the intensity of his gestures and the flare of his nostrils, I knew his words weren't going to be the tender apology Phoebe predicted.

I braced myself.

His eyes narrowed to reptilian slits when he spotted me, but he waited for me to sit down before delivering his reproach.

"Miriam, how could you have behaved like that?" His brow crimpled with anger; he spoke slowly as if he had to concentrate on each word. Even so, his voice quivered with barely-controlled anger. "First you left the *tribunal* without saying a word just as the fans were uncoiling their rage over the death of Orcus—"

Actually, I'd left shortly before that, not that he'd have noticed. Anyway, the detail was hardly worth pressing, so I continued to listen with feigned patience as I watched a black fly circle above the window sill.

"—But then, to make matters worse, you left the stadium altogether without even thanking the procurator or saying goodbye to Eran. I've asked you repeatedly to make friends with my brother, but instead you seem to go out of your way to antagonize him."

I couldn't face telling him about Binyamin. Still, I owed him a somewhat truthful account of why I didn't go back to the *tribunal*. But for starters, I decided to apologize.

"When I saw you on my way back from the latrines, I thought you'd be able to thank Eran for me. He knew I'd been feeling ill since the reception. But as far as the procurator is concerned, you're right. I was rude. Fortunately, I can't imagine my lapse spoiling his evening, but yes, it could affect how he feels about Eran. And for that I'm truly sorry."

I wasn't sure how sorry I was, but I let my voice fall so he'd think I was.

In the meantime, the fly landed on the edge of a slat, where a ray of light painted its wings with rainbows.

"But I want to explain why I couldn't go back to the *tribunal*, why I needed to get away from the crowds."

Be careful, I warned myself. *Don't tell him too much.* Remember, he still doesn't know (and you don't want to tell him) that the League's scrolls once found their way to Noah's house, where Drakon had access to them. So he couldn't know Drakon was the one who copied his recipe and sold it to Eran (among others). Consequently Judah would never understand why Drakon, once he suspected I'd found out, would hatch a diabolical scheme to murder me.

So I just reached inside the satchel.

Shifting in his chair, Judah raked his hands through his hair while I unwrapped the *sica* and laid it on a stripe of light.

"So, what's this got to do with anything?" Judah asked, leaning back and folding his arms across his chest.

"When I was coming back from the latrines but before I saw you, I suddenly realized I'd lost my sense of direction. In that moment of panic, I spun around to backtrack. That maneuver foiled a *Sicarius's* attack."

"Gee, Miriam, you should have told me."

The exasperation had leached out of his voice, but I was too aggrieved to respond to his concern.

"Why? So you could apprehend the assassin with your bare hands, something the full force of Rome has been unable to do?" I heard my voice getting shrill, so I took a breath, but the air, as it scraped against my throat, sounded like a snort. "Believe me," I said, waggling my head. "He was gone before I could turn around.

"Besides, you seemed oblivious to my welfare from my arrival at the reception to the games themselves. If it weren't for Eran, I'd have felt hopelessly alone."

"Listen, Miriam, that was Eran's idea not mine. He asked

me to stay away from you. He said he wanted to be the one to look after you, to show you a Caesarea you'd never forget."

"Well, he certainly succeeded in doing that." I'm not sure Judah caught my irony, but rather than divert the discussion, I pointed to the *sica*. "Do you recognize the emblem on the handle?"

"I've seen it before, but I can't recall where." Judah gazed into the middle distance. Then he bowed his head and, with his fingertips at his temples, closed his eyes.

So I turned my attention back to the fly. This time it was buzzing from the underside of the sill.

"Think back to when you were in Eran's study searching through his ring keys to find the one that would open the compartment where he kept the scroll. Among them—you said you counted ten—there was an agate seal ring with an emblem just like this."

His gaze snapped back to meet mine. "Yes," he said, nodding curtly. "Now I remember. The seal ring stood out because it was bronze. The rest of the rings were iron. So why is that important?"

"Well, it means there's a connection, however tenuous, between Eran and this *sica*. I personally think he crafted this one, perhaps even others—"

"—What on earth are you talking about?" A column of fire shot up his neck and ignited his face. "There you go again, jumping to conclusions. You come up with a million wild theories, and in each case, my brother is the villain."

On its face, I couldn't deny his claim, but it still hurt me to hear him say it.

"Okay, okay," I said, my arms spread, my palms patting down the air. "But let me show you one more thing, the candlestick Eran gave me when I visited his shop."

He drummed his fingers on the edge of the table. "Really, is this necessary? I can see where you're going with this, that my brother is the archenemy of Rome, the ringleader of the *Sicarii*, the terrorist they've been searching for all these years. Next you'll try to convince me he's been spying on Alexander, using his influence to temper the procurator's decrees and when he can, to fleece him out of a pinch of gold here and there so he can save the peasants' farms—"

"—But Judah, just look at the color of this candlestick and compare it to the *sica*."

"Okay. So they're both brass," he said, stirring the air with a flick of his hand.

"But they're a distinctive color of brass. I've tested them, Judah, the *sica* and the candlestick. Their brass is made from the same unusually high proportion of calamine. Eran not only cast this candlestick, he compounded the brass for it too. I saw the crucibles in his shop myself. All I'm saying is he compounded the brass for this *sica* as well."

His outrage radiated like waves of heat.

"Look, Judah, Eran is mixed up with the *Sicarii*. Why they've targeted me for assassination, I have no idea"—at least that's what I told him. "And by the way, I also think I was the intended victim when they killed the Judean matron. Her *sica* had this same emblem."

"Miriam, I can't sit here and listen to your accusations anymore. First you come to Caesarea obsessed with the provenance of Eran's recipe, something that's frankly none of your business. Then you repeatedly abuse my brother's hospitality even as you blame him for his indignation and impugn his sanity. And now you charge him with consorting with terrorists. Perhaps it would be better for all of us—and certainly for me—if you returned to Alexandria at once."

Next he shoved the table aside, sprung from his chair, and lurched toward the door. Along the way, he careened against the sideboard, leaving in his wake a cascading arc of bones and gristle, a rill of froth zigzagging between the tiles, and a cacophony of pinwheeling cutlery, smashing crockery, and shattering glassware. And, as if that wasn't embarrassing enough, before storming out of the dining room, he cast one last searing scowl in my direction.

I watched the fly dive into the rill of froth while I heard Judah's *calcei* stomp across the portico.

Vacant moments slid past me while my body turned to stone, and my mind floated above it. When at last it rejoined my body, I packed up the satchel, threaded my arm through its strap, and toddled up the stairs to the dim, melancholy *cella* as if I'd just learned to walk. With Phoebe having gone to see Bion, the room was empty save for the growing shadows, the dull throb of afternoon heat, and the stench of the stable yard.

Still numb, I let go of the satchel, groped for my cot, and fell onto its scratchy coverlet while the room swayed, and echoes of Judah's voice pulsed through my head. I must have drifted into a thin sleep because I kept seeing a flickering image of Judah—or was it Drakon?—pelting me with luncheon scraps. In the dream, I dropped my chin and cradled my head, but a barrage of shattered glassware struck my temples, igniting a flash of pain and unleashing a torrent of blood.

And then Phoebe was leaning over me, pulling me out of my stupor. When I opened my eyes, the room was drenched in shadows, but she'd lit the candelabrum by my cot. As its flame burned away the vestiges of my imagination, I raised my head from the pillow and rubbed the sleepiness from my eyes, never expecting she'd be bringing me more startling news.

Chapter 25

Tuesday Early Evening

"MIRIAM, YOU HAVE to get up. Bion is waiting for us in the dining room. Drakon was stabbed in the Forum this afternoon."

"What?"

"Yes, it's true. He died before our very eyes, before Bion's anyway."

"How did it happen?"

Phoebe plopped down at the foot of my cot, shed her sandals, and then drew up her knees and locked her arms around them. When she inhaled deeply and swallowed hard, I knew I was in for the full account, every embroidered detail.

Her lips twitching into a satisfied smile, she was enjoying her moment as my loyal scout.

"Well, Bion and I were in the Forum, walking to the textile shop where Drakon bought that satchel. Bion wants to replace the scrim that separates his office from the retail space. He says it's tattered. Of course we noticed the procurator's litter there, the one Drakon uses—I mean used to use—the one with the fancy bronze cabin. The *pedisequi* always clear so much space, as if they're escorting the emperor himself. But then, all of a sudden, we heard a chorus of screams and watched a wave of commotion rock the crowd.

"Bion paddled through the ring of chaos in time to see a man prone on the pavement, both hands clapped to his mouth, a dagger stuck in his back. And then, after one final spurt of foam gushed through his waxy fingers, he slumped into the puddle of his own blood. Based on the gory print of a hand in a diagonal smear along the side of the litter, Bion figured the man must have collapsed sideways and reached for the litter before pitching to the pavement."

I'd gotten used to my Phoebe's vivid descriptions. Still, I had to struggle with my waning patience.

"Soon after, a wedge of infantrymen converged on the litter, their pot helmets, iron cuirasses, and drawn swords flashing against their bright red tunics. The soldier at the vertex burst forward. Tall and lanky, his ferret face poised high above the others, he surveyed the crowd with his calculating eyes. Next he tucked his sword into the sheath hanging from his belt and sank to the pavement with the grace of a snake. After that, he let go of his shield and straddled the body to pull out the dagger.

"He must have recognized the corpse right away because he immediately told the others that Drakon, the procurator's head scribe, had been stabbed and was dead."

A rush of relief flowed through me.

"Bion understood the soldier's rudimentary Latin, which is more than I can say despite Hector's best efforts. Then, according to Bion, the soldier asked in Latin and Aramaic before finally in Greek whether any of us had seen the attack. Halfheartedly, of course. He knew no one would risk getting implicated in a murder, of the procurator's head scribe no less.

"No one, that is, except an old Greek slave so stooped it's a wonder he could see anything above his feet. Perhaps the prospect of a reward stirred his tongue. Anyway, he contributed nothing new. He reported only that he'd seen a dark, fully-mantled figure slip out from the shadows, brush against the victim's cloak, and then disappear. He punctuated his account with a gnarled index finger, pointing first toward an arcaded gallery and then toward a graffiti-lined alley so thick with waste that it was more of a gutter than anything else. As you might expect, the other witnesses, as if on cue, then turned to each other, nodded, and growled in agreement.

"As soon as the soldiers left, Bion and I forgot about the scrim and went back to his shop, where he drew a picture of the dagger for me. It was a *sica* all right, short, curved, and brass, and guess what? It had the same crude outline engraved on its handle.

"That's when I knew we should tell you right away."

And that's when the relief curdled in my veins. If someone with that kind of *sica* killed Drakon, then who, if not Drakon, was trying to kill me? And why?

I DIDN'T WANT to sit in the dining room again. I was sure Judah's mess had been cleared, but I wanted to talk where the three of us could not be overheard. So, accompanied by an orange sun hovering over the sea, the dreary beat of the surf, a shifting sea breeze, and the calls of birds claiming their roost for the night, we walked the short distance to Bion's shop, treading on the crisp shadows of the *cardo*'s mansions and monuments, arcades and tenements. Whenever I'd glance at Phoebe, my eyes would catch the evening's last glow rimming the right side of her face as she walked alongside me, Bion a few steps behind.

The shop was dark, but Bion needed only a minute to light some oil lamps and scatter them about his office. He put a few Herodian lamps next to the busts on the shelves and a large, circular Roman lamp in the center of the rosewood table. We took our seats around the table just as we had more than a week ago, Phoebe and Bion across from each other with me next to Phoebe. But this time Bion unrolled his drawing of the dagger that killed Drakon. Just as Phoebe had said, it was a *sica* with a crude outline of a radiant sun on its handle, an exact match to the other two *sicae*, the Judean matron's and mine, and Eran's seal ring.

"Listen, Bion, I need to ask you for another favor. Now that Drakon is dead, I want to claim the contents of his box in the Public Records Office. But we'd have to hurry, before his death can be registered and the box sealed."

His neck lengthened.

"I know you don't have the token, but I think we can trick the clerk. After all, Phoebe knows the box number and can describe the token."

I caught Phoebe's nod through the corner of my eye.

"Just tell the clerk your purse was stolen, your token was inside the purse, and you want to claim the contents of your box before the thief can.

"Tell him the box contains a tablet and scrolls of the finest Egyptian papyrus. We can't be sure how many are there or even how many tablets, but if we keep it simple, we can assume Drakon didn't add or remove anything since Phoebe followed him two days ago. Then Phoebe can estimate the size of the box based on her glimpse into the vault, and I can figure out how many scrolls it could hold."

According to Judah, Eran's copy was a complete record of his and Saul's recipe, no more and no less, and I wasn't about to forget the size of that scroll when two years ago, recovering it nearly cost me my life.

"So then you can just subtract the five she saw him take out. Anyway, there'll be at least one. Drakon wouldn't have sold his last copy.

"But wait, here comes the daunting part: Of course, the clerk might refuse to hand over the contents without the token. But suppose he believes you. Soon enough with Drakon's murder, the authorities will investigate. Drakon's token will be found. They'll go to the Public Records Office, and when they see his box is empty, they'll question the clerks. The clerk who served you might remember you and describe you to the authorities. But all in all, I think he'd be more likely to deny any part in the transaction.

"Another danger: If Drakon was killed because of the scrolls, then you too could be at risk for having even one of them in your possession, however briefly."

Bion nodded to show he understood. Then, with his elbow on the table, his chin resting on the back of his folded hand, and his brow drawn low, he blinked into the flame of the Roman lamp while a silence settled around him. Finally, he raised his eyes, lowered his arm, and faced Phoebe four square. She must have given him a sign because after that, his expression softened.

With his eyes still focused on Phoebe, he leaned back, folded his arms across his chest, and took a deep breath. "I'll be there first thing in the morning," he said.

I tiptoed out, a fierce self-loathing sweeping over me for jeopardizing Bion's safety in pursuit of my own lost cause. I found no comfort even from the fire of Drusion the way I used to in Alexandria from the Pharos Lighthouse.

Chapter 26

Wednesday Morning

I AWOKE THE next morning with my head throbbing and the foul taste of guilt coating my tongue. All night long in my dreams, I kept trying to redo the events of the past, beginning with that Shabbat in Alexandria two years ago. If only I'd told Noah the truth, that I wasn't going to marry him, then he wouldn't have filched the League's scrolls from my cubby, experimented with Saul and Judah's recipe, and died choking on the fumes. And I wouldn't have had to lie to Judah about the whereabouts of the scrolls when I couldn't return them.

And Drakon couldn't have copied the recipe and sold it to Eran and who knows how many others. And I wouldn't have had to come to Caesarea in a futile attempt to recover it. And then I wouldn't have caused the death of the Judean matron, alienated Judah, and ensnared Bion in my desperate attempt to salvage what I could of the Almighty's Secrets.

Instead, in my reinvented reality, Noah and I would still be friends, and Judah and I would be planning a future together. During the day, we'd work together in his shop, fashioning experimental apparatus and perfecting recipes to transmute base metals into gold, all the while keeping the Divine Secrets safe from the Gentiles. And during the night, our bodies entwined, we'd lose ourselves in a slow-burning passion until, intoxicated with pleasure and flooded with relief, we'd fall asleep, our bodies folded together, our lips murmuring each other's name.

But that version was no longer possible.

And so, when I awoke, I wanted only to dive under the coverlet, sink into a sweet doze, and find my way back to that Shabbat when my only worry was my betrothal to Noah. But

Phoebe's footfalls thumping up the stairs two at a time denied me that opportunity. So I sat up and stretched my limbs just as she burst through the door.

"Bion left for the Public Records Office a little while ago," she said, catching her breath, her eyes flashing with excitement, her words tumbling together. "He wants us to wait for him in his shop."

I reluctantly rubbed the sleep from my eyes, but they still felt gritty.

"Come on, Miriam, get up. You look a hundred years old with the rumpled bedding stamped on your face. Besides, Bion could come back with Drakon's things any minute. Don't you want to see what that swindler had stashed in his box?"

Actually, I didn't. I knew what Bion would find. And I regretted having sent him. Maybe he could help prevent the dissemination of a few more scrolls, but what difference would that really make? The damage had been done. Was retrieving those last few copies really worth risking Bion's life and Phoebe's happiness?

"Okay. Okay," I groaned, dragging myself out of bed against the forces of guilt, which weighed me down like a stone.

"What's the matter with you this morning, Miriam? Can't you move any faster?"

But I knew better than to answer. I just stood like a statue while she bathed and dressed me. All the while she chattered on about how she went to the shop early to help Bion rehearse his story: How she described the satchel Drakon carried (new, plain linen, about a foot and a half long, and with a thick strap) and where he bought it (at the textile shop in the middle of the Forum). And how she drew the token for him exactly as she remembered it (square, lead, as thick as a coin with the numeral XIV embossed on both sides). And how she estimated the size of the box (about a quarter of the size of the acacia cabinet under the busts in Bion's office). I hardly paid attention until I heard her mention breakfast. Suddenly, I was famished.

So much for the foul taste of guilt.

"I've already had breakfast," she said, "but we can order

something for you from Otho's, and I can wait for it. What would you like?"

"What did I have last time? Never mind. I can't remember whether I even liked it."

"I'm sure you loved it." Her voice was oiled with certainty as she crossed the room to pull out a tunic from the rattan chest.

But then, a moment later, her voice was barbed with impatience. "I'm waiting for you to stand up straight and hold out your arms. How else do you expect me to fasten this tunic?"

"Well, just get me an order of yogurt, dates, and black tea." I figured they would slide down easily enough.

"Sounds good. Come to think of it, I'll get that for myself too."

"I thought you already had breakfast."

"I did, but no sense going hungry. You never know how long we might have to wait for Bion."

How right she was.

THE SUN TOUCHED us as soon as we stepped out of the inn and onto the *cardo*, its light blanching the very mansions and monuments, arcades and tenements that it draped in pearly shadows last evening. I watched the tops of the cypress trees sway in the cool breeze and felt the warming cobbles through the soles of my sandals as we picked our way around the peddlers and pushcarts in a shared silence, our ears too beset by the hubbub of traffic, the brays of street vendors, the haggling of shoppers, and the whines of beggars to converse.

I left Phoebe at Otho's to place the order at his streetside counter. Before crossing to Bion's shop, I had to pause for a litter carrying two stout matrons to turn from the *cardo* onto the *decumanus*. While waiting, I wondered whether Bion was back yet from the Public Records Office, whether he was able to claim the contents of the box, and if so, what I could learn from his find. Would I come across a document to prove that Drakon had been the one trying to kill me? And would I find out why? Had someone hired him? Who (and another why)? And would a new assassin take his place?

A twinge of dread rippled down my spine like a thousand tiny dagger pricks, but I took a deep breath, leaned against the column of an arcade, and concentrated instead on retying the ribbons that laced my sandals. After that, I was ready to cross the *decumanus*. When I reached Bion's shop, I paused with my hand on the door handle to brace myself for what I might learn inside.

Both clerks were occupied with customers. The bald one with the lopsided head—Phoebe told me his name is Thoth—circulated among them, answering their questions or directing them to one of the display cases. The yellow-eyed one—his name is Galen—was standing at a counter near the front of the shop collecting the money for each purchase. But first, depending on the customer's currency, he'd calculate the cost on an abacus with the ease and efficiency of the best money changers in the Forum. He might be paid in Greek drachmas, Roman denarii, Tyrian zuzim, or the aniconic bronze coins the Romans struck for the Jews. And every once in a while, he'd even come across an old bronze prutah left over from the Hasmonean dynasty, which he'd accept along with the customer's other coins.

As busy as they were, they noticed me as soon as I entered the shop. Galen glanced my way, rapidly blinking a hello with his lashless lids. Thoth pointed me toward the office with a jerk of his lopsided head. But I knew Bion wasn't back yet. With the shop this crowded, he'd surely be attending to customers along with his clerks.

So much for Phoebe's rushing me.

I pulled aside the scrim and entered Bion's office. The shutters on the window were closed, so only a few fingers of light could poke through the slats and drip their gold across the carpet. I folded the panels back to welcome what remained of the morning sun, hung my himation on the ear of a chair, and stood near the window so I could at least pretend to be in my favorite places in Alexandria.

But the painting of the Park of Pan, the site the early Ptolomies created for their goatlike god, pierced me with an unexpected sadness. I remembered how, after seeing Judah in the agora, I'd climb its fir-cone-shaped hill, spiraling around until I reached its summit. Then I'd look out at the magnificent view of my city, at the walls that could no longer contain its sprawl, and imagine my own future expanding beyond my father's boundaries to make a life with Judah possible. As my eyes glazed over and blurred the painting into a muddle of lines and colors, I realized Judah was right. It was time for me to return to Alexandria.

And by tomorrow night, I'd wish I'd left sooner.

OF ALL THINGS, I smelled muffins like the ones our cook would make at home. Turning around, I saw Phoebe balancing a wooden tray as Thoth held the scrim aside for her.

"Here, Miriam. Take this, and I'll set the table."

My nose was right. In addition to the yogurt, dates, and tea, Phoebe brought us a basket of hot coriander muffins along with a lavish assortment of cheeses and nuts. While I unloaded the tray, she located Bion's table linens in one of the marble-topped cabinets. In no time, she had Otho's crockery precisely arranged on a starched white cloth trimmed with lace.

"See, Miriam, this is like old times," she said, sitting down to face the scrim so she could watch for Bion. "Remember when we used to have breakfast under the canopy of your father's roof garden? That's why I got us the coriander muffins. Not that I expect these to be as good as the ones we got at home, but still . . ."

Before her voice dribbled into silence, I noticed its huskiness. Was she thinking about going back to Alexandria, or on the contrary, did she yearn to stay here with Bion?

"You know, Phoebe, we talked many times in Alexandria about Papa's willingness to pay the tax for your manumission. And you always said you'd never want to leave our family, that you liked your life just the way it was. But now that you've found Bion again, maybe you've changed your mind and would rather stay here. I could arrange to manumit you from Alexandria and ship your things—"

I was mentally preparing the papers, paying the tax, and

shipping her goods as I paced back and forth across the front of the room, my head down, my tented fingers pressed against my chin.

"I've been thinking about that too. Bion has asked me to stay and marry him, and he's offered to pay you for my freedom, but I'm not ready yet. You'd be so far away. I couldn't count on ever seeing—"

"Of course, we'd see each—"

"Now if he were willing to relocate to Alexan—"

"Could that really happen?"

"I don't know. He loves Alexandria. And he still has his connections at the Great Library. They could help him establish a successful business. And maybe he'd even keep his shop here for Thoth and Galen to run. But if I did ask him to come to Alexandria, I'd have to be willing to marry him. And I'm not sure about that either."

I remembered my own quandary about marrying Noah.

She gulped the tea as if she'd been wandering in the desert and then snatched a muffin with one hand and a fistful of almonds with the other. A second muffin later, lifting her chin, she cleared her throat.

"I don't know what came over me, Miriam," she said, brushing away the trail of crumbs she'd left on the tablecloth. "I felt like I hadn't eaten for days."

"Maybe you're worried about Bion."

She nodded slowly, staring vacantly into the middle distance as she worked her teeth with her tongue.

"He's been gone a long time." I tried to keep the alarm out of my voice, but judging by the stiffening of her body, I think my monotone frightened her even more. The Public Records Office was only a block away, and he'd been gone for hours. The heat had already swallowed up the brisk morning air, and the rectangle of light framed by the window had faded to a dull sheen.

I thought of getting a scroll from a display case and reading to pass the time—I never did finish *The Clouds*, and I was sure Bion had a copy—but I was too restless to focus on anything. So I reached above the cabinet for his Roman lamp and then walked over to close the shutters.

"Leave the shutters open, Miriam. You can't fool me. I know the eastern light is dwindling. You said you were hungry. I got you what you wanted. So sit down and eat."

I told you Phoebe could be officious.

I sat across from her and nibbled on a date while I sipped my tepid tea and watched the morning wear away. Somehow I managed to drink the tea and eat the yogurt while she consumed most of the rest, leaving only a muffin, the rest of the dates, and some of the cheese for Bion in case he was hungry when he returned.

We decided to pass the time by cleaning Bion's office, not that it was dirty, far from it, but we needed something to do. So Phoebe asked Thoth to bring us a broom and some cleaning rags—he protested mildly, but Phoebe prevailed—and she asked him to return the tray of crockery to Otho's, which he undertook graciously. Phoebe dusted while I swept, shook out the tablecloth, and refilled the oil lamps. The tasks did little, however, to enliven our sagging spirits. Each of us in turn and with increasing dread watched the light from the window flatten still more to a lifeless gray.

Chapter 27

Wednesday Afternoon

PHOEBE HEARD his voice first. Or maybe she recognized his footfalls because suddenly her features sharpened, and she cocked her ear toward the scrim. A moment later, we heard Bion greeting his clerks and the few customers in the shop.

It was well into the afternoon. We'd been sitting across from each other, both of us fidgeting, Phoebe hunched over, her anxious hands gripping mine, my knuckles throbbing from the pressure. But then, as soon as the scrim fluttered, she let go of my hands and stood up so quickly I thought her chair would topple over. I turned and also rose to my feet but more slowly. The strain of waiting had stiffened my knees and wrapped my legs in cramps.

I'm not so sure I would have recognized the dark figure that passed through the scrim had we not heard his voice and been expecting him. He was wrapped in a long black silk cloak, his face obscured by its hood, his arms tucked inside the folds of its skirt, one hand grasping the strap of a new, rather full but otherwise unremarkable linen satchel.

"We were so worried." Phoebe's voice was both a whisper and a sigh.

"I'm so very sorry, my precious. After I left you, I thought of one more ploy to optimize our chances for success." He was leaning toward her, his voice as soothing as an offshore breeze. "I knew you'd be worried, but I also knew I'd have just this one opportunity to recover the scrolls."

He laid the satchel down at the head of the table. I tried to peer inside it, but its opening was positioned toward him. He unfastened his cloak—Galen materialized instantly to take it

145

away—and pulled over a chair so he could address both of us. Then he settled into it, took a breath so deep his nostrils flared, and rested his forearms on the edge of the table.

His bloodshot eyes, red-rimmed lids, and sagging cheeks told me he hadn't slept much the previous night.

Just as Phoebe set out a plate for him with the muffin and what was left of the cheeses and dates, Galen returned with a glass of steaming tea. The most nerve-racking wait of all was for him to finish eating so I could hear his story.

"I LEFT YOU this morning, my darling, intent on going directly to the Public Records Office with the number of the box and shape of the token fixed in my memory."

As if pulled by the same string, Phoebe and I angled our bodies toward him.

"But before I'd even crossed the *cardo*, I realized I didn't look anything like the lean-faced corpse sprawled on the pavement in the Forum. I had to do something to mask my own appearance and resemble his more closely.

"Mindful of the time pressure—I knew I had to get to the Public Records Office before Drakon's box was sealed—I nevertheless first scurried to the textile shop he frequented to order a cloak like his. I paid a premium to get them to make it up for me at once and call for me at Vesta's Teahouse when it was done. At the same time, I bought a satchel similar to the one my darling saw Drakon carrying last Sunday morning."

As soon as he said "my darling," I could hear a slight tremor in his voice. He'd turned to look at Phoebe, and for that barely perceptible moment, his eyes embraced hers. Then facing me and swallowing, he continued.

"While waiting at Vesta's, I was consumed with self-doubt. Shouldn't I have followed your instructions and gone directly to the Public Records Office? That question kept worming through my brain. But Drakon had gone in the morning. So wouldn't I have a better of chance of getting a different clerk if I went in the afternoon?

"I remembered Galen and Thoth telling me that the new clerks work in the afternoon. The senior clerks don't want that shift; they complain the hall gets too hot. And the administrator reasons that with the afternoon's thinning crowds and shorter lines, the new clerks have more time to learn their craft. But doesn't that mean they'd be closely supervised? That they'd adhere to the standard procedure for each transaction?"

Bion lifted his glass and took a sip of tea.

"Then again, the advantage of my going in the morning would be that the clerks have to hustle, perhaps to the point of being careless. But I'd also run a greater risk of encountering people I know. And finally, I wondered whether I was over-analyzing the situation, whether I was obsessing to the point of paralysis so that even when I got the cloak, I'd invent yet another reason to delay."

His head swiveled back and forth between Phoebe and me as he explained his dilemma.

"As you can see, a million questions swirled through my brain. But, in the end, I decided to stay and wait for the cloak.

"So, my poor darling," he said, reaching for Phoebe's hand. "While you were worrying, I was breathing in the smell of fried onions with an undercurrent of dirty feet, staring at a plate of boiled eggs, and drinking an indifferent tea that reminded me of the muddy waters of the Nile."

He knew how to make my Phoebe smile.

"Well, after all that fretting, yours and mine, something quite unforeseeable happened anyway."

I slid to the edge of my chair.

"The hall was as hot as Helphaistos's smithy and nearly deserted when I passed through its double doors. Just the administrator and some clerks, a few businessmen, and a spidery old woman I recognized as the *hospita* from The Hercules. When I heard my heels fill the hall with their echo, I softened my tread and lined up behind her. Only two service windows were open, and I wanted to avoid the businessmen, who were moving as one toward the other window. Any one of them might have met me in the shop or known Drakon.

"And that's when my luck blossomed albeit, I regret to say, at the expense of that poor crone. She fainted, probably from the heat. In the sliver of a moment, she crumpled to the floor. The coins in her still-open purse clanged across the marble floor and rolled about as the administrator rushed to her side with a flask. And there I was, standing at the service window before a stunned, snaggle-toothed clerk, who reached out to me with sinewy arms, eager to complete the transaction so he could show his supervisor he knew how to take care of the crone."

"See, Miriam, I told you Isis is watching over us."

"So, as soon as I told the clerk the box number, he didn't even ask for the token. He just hustled over to the vault, pulled out box XIV, and plunked it on the counter whereupon I packed the contents into the satchel, rapidly but not in haste, and left."

BION PAUSED IN his narrative while Galen served us a platter of apricots, oranges, and plums. With sweet relief surging through my veins, seeping into my limbs, and softening my face into almost a smile, I felt an intense debt of gratitude and a rumble of hunger. But as I bit into my second plum, needles of anxiety were already pricking my innards. What, beyond what I already knew, could I glean from Drakon's box?

And so, after Galen cleared the table and glided out with the empty platter, and after I expressed my deepest thanks to Bion, I asked him to show me what he brought. Yes, he'd gotten everything from the box, all in all two scrolls and a tablet, probably the one Phoebe saw Drakon write on last Sunday.

Bion stood, unpacked the satchel, stacking its contents before me, and then, in an unusually insistent tone and with a squint that could have been a wink, he told Phoebe he wanted her advice on replacing the scrim. Would she accompany him to the Forum but this time to a different textile shop?

That's how I found myself alone with the remnants of the very intrigue that had brought me to Caesarea. Here my life had been threatened twice, a Judean matron had been killed in my place, and a scoundrel, perhaps himself even a murderer, had been assassinated. My relationship with Judah was in a shambles, and I'd had a distressing reunion with my brother, but with the courage of a faithful new friend, the devotion of my loyal Phoebe, and the grace of G-d, I'd managed to survive. And so, with a smile expanding inside me, I gave thanks to the Almighty for His intervention.

And then I was ready to examine the scrolls. With damp, trembling hands, I unrolled them both. Then, taking Bion's globe from his workbench and hunching over their penultimate panels, I checked whether they were identical to each other and to the one from Eran as I remembered it. Using the globe and the techniques Bion had shown me, I compared the slant of the strokes, the color of the ink (and its occasional splotches and nubs), the nicks from the *calamus*, and the texture of the papyrus. I knew at that moment that Drakon had made these copies as well as Eran's. And my hands trembled all the more.

Next I picked up the tablet. It looked like a record of Drakon's sales. Alongside each customer's name was a numeral presumably indicating how many copies each had bought. Eran's name, for example, was followed by the numeral I, and Godarz, the only Parthian name (but written in Greek characters), was followed by the numeral V. Among the score of customers, only Eran had purchased a single copy.

That was the evidence. Period. I was no closer to finding out who'd been trying to kill me or when he would strike again. And when I realized that, my whole body drooped as if it were boneless.

The other question was who killed Drakon. Did the *Sicarii* kill him as a warning to the procurator, the Jew (if you'd still call him one) who bows lower than all others to Rome? Or did Tiberius Julius Alexander himself have Drakon killed for dealing in alchemical recipes? Or was he killed by an enraged customer who'd learned that Drakon, despite his pledge, had sold the recipe to others? If so, then Drakon's tablet could be a list of suspects.

And then it struck me. Drakon was killed with a *sica*, but not just any *sica*. Its handle bore the symbol of a radiant sun. Certainly the procurator's soldiers didn't have access to a dagger like that. Nor would most of Drakon's customers. Perhaps not even most of the *Sicarii*.

Then I knew. And the fear buzzed through me. I was on the list of unfinished business. With my head whirling, my blood throbbing, and my skin feverish, I rolled up the scrolls, gathered them up with the tablet, and packed them into Bion's satchel. Next I untied my sash and raised it so it spanned my back under my arms and opened across my chest. I threaded the sash through the strap of the satchel and then retied it so the contents rested against my belly. Lastly, I wrapped the himation around my thickened body. That's how I lumbered back to the inn, checking the long shadows in my wake for the ripple of a cloak while pretending to admire a vase in a stall, inspect the fruit on a pushcart, or pick a pebble out of my sandal. And wishing Binyamin was here to protect me.

Chapter 28

Thursday Morning

"PHOEBE, ARE YOU up yet?" I whispered. The first needles of light poking through the shutters were stabbing me in the eye.

"Why aren't you sleeping?" she asked in the midst of an extravagant yawn. Sitting up, throwing her head back, and stretching like a cat, she planted her feet on the floor and shambled toward the washbasin.

"I'm going to book passage for us today on the next ship to Alexandria, that is if you still want to go—"

"Yes, yes, I'm sure—" She tossed the words over her shoulder while she searched for fresh towels.

"And I need to say good-bye to Judah," I said, leaning back on my elbows and closing my eyes.

As much as I longed to see him, I also dreaded it. No matter how I planned the conversation, he could fly into a rage, once again spitting angry words at me, leaving me no opportunity to convince him that Eran was not only dangerous to others but in danger himself. He killed Alexander's head scribe! Judah must leave immediately. With no protection under Roman law, he could be arrested, tortured until he incriminated Eran as the assassin (or even himself as an accomplice), and summarily executed.

So I had to make him listen. I knew from the seal ring, the brass candlestick, and the *sicae* that Eran had either killed Drakon himself or hired someone to do it, and the only difference between Drakon and me was that I'd been lucky enough to dodge the dagger. Twice. But only with the tablet could I prove Eran had a motive for killing Drakon.

"So where do you want to go first?" Phoebe directed her

question to the towels.

"Eran's house. I think I better go there right after breakfast. Eran will be in his shop by then, Jabin probably with him. So I'll have a chance to be alone with Judah, to show him the tablet and say good-bye.

"Listen, you might want to see Bion then too, before his shop gets busy. And if you do, you can give him back his satchel. By the way, would you like to invite him to come with us to Alexandria?"

"Oh, no, Miriam. I'm not ready for that, but I'd be willing to resume the correspondence we had when he first left Alexandria."

"Okay. So this afternoon, I'll book passage for the two of us. For now though, you heat up the *calamistrum* and call for the *puer*. I'll pack up our satchel with Drakon's tablet and order breakfast for, let's say, in about an hour. I'm going to need that much time to prepare to see Judah."

I sensed the three white-robed Fates propelling me toward the conclusion of my business in Caesarea. Little did I know what they had in mind.

BY THE TIME Phoebe finished fussing with the willful ringlets along the nape of my neck and dressed me in a short-sleeved blue linen tunic, we were ready to sit down to a hearty breakfast of black tea, sweet oranges, and steamed fish garnished with olives and spiked with hot pepper. I remember we stuffed ourselves like soldiers, as if there was no tomorrow.

And by the time we stepped into the street, the sun had swallowed up the early morning coolness, and the shimmer off the buildings was forcing our eyes to the pavement. With the satchel hanging from my shoulder and my forearm bracing it against my hip, we threaded our way through the thickening crowds to Bion's shop, where I left Phoebe after stopping in myself to thank Bion again.

Then, instead of continuing along the *Cardo Maximus* and turning east on the *Decumanus Maximus*, I took the side streets to avoid the congestion so close to the Forum: the stalled carts, litters, and drays, the harried throngs, the snaking lines, and most of all, the assassins I imagined lurking in the shadow of every portico, the shade of every alleyway, and the plume of every cloud of dust.

I passed palm trees, their fronds arching over the walkways, and stands of young, conic-crowned Lebanon cedars. I peeked over lattice fences shielding bowers of roses, beds of foaming foliage, and pools of floating lotus lilies, their delicately-scented flowers unfurled for their morning pollinators. And I counted the slanting rectangles of light leaning on the frescoed east-facing garden walls.

But as soon as I turned the corner onto Eran's block, what began as a vague disquiet and a mild prick of anxiety bloomed into a sharp foreboding and an irrepressible dread of entering that house. A bilious scum bubbled up from my gut along with all the formless self-doubts of my childhood. Even the sunshine became a burden on my shoulders, a weight I couldn't shrug off.

I crossed Eran's lush lawns to the peony-lined walkway and waved to the two houseboys spraying iridescent beads of water on the beds fringing the estate. I knocked on the double doors, timidly I admit. With no one answering, I gingerly turned the handles. The doors swung open, and I found myself once again in the atrium staring at the Etruscan *hydriae* that flank the doors to Eran's study. I wondered which one housed the reptile today. Taking a seat by the *impluvium*, I placed the satchel next to me on the bench. Once settled, I checked my reflection in the water and fluffed my matted hair. What a mess! My ringlets had drooped and were sticking to the clammy sweat dotting the nape of my neck.

And I could smell the stink of my own fear.

I waited.

Still no one.

I called for Judah.

Louder.

Then for anyone.

"Helloooo. Anybody home?"

I craned my neck and stretched my gaze into the *triclinium*, but its forest of lamp stands obscured the interior.

That's when I heard the rustle of silk.

And the scuff of slippers.

And the hammering of my heart.

"What a delightful surprise, my dear. I was just thinking of you." His voice was as thick and sweet as honey. "And a moment later, here you are. Amazing!" Probably wondering how I got in or whether he'd suddenly acquired a magic power, he scratched his head with his ring-studded fingers.

And parted his curls.

His stain peeked out.

"Well, Judah must have left the doors unlocked. He's been doing that lately. Anyway, I hope I didn't startle you." His lips thinned to an icy line while his obsidian eyes flickered with malevolence.

Another stream of scum spewed into my mouth, but with a hard swallow, I managed to suppress the burgeoning gag.

His eyes riveted on my throat. "Don't tell me you're ill again."

"I was just surprised to see you. I'm looking for Judah."

"*Tsk, tsk, tsk.* You just missed him." He closed his eyes and waggled his head in a gesture I recognized as irony, not the sympathy I'd once thought. "He's in the shop this morning. I'm to relieve him later, but I have an appointment at the palace first. Alexander has asked me to submit my designs for the medallions he'll present at the next games."

"And Jabin?"

"He's with Judah, as usual minding the accounts. It's just you and I, my dear."

"Well, I can come back another time, you know, if it's more convenient," I stammered.

"No, of course not. Why should you do that?"

A coil of silence tightened around us.

I heard a weight shift in one of the *hydriae*.

We sat as still as statues. I didn't know what to say or where to pitch my eyes, so I examined the backs of my hands as if some hint were written on them.

Eran broke the silence with a prim cough.

My gaze snapped back.

His eyes ensnared mine.

I felt his mind prying into mine.

Pearls of sweat escaped from beneath his wig, trickled over his stain, and made it glisten.

"What do you have in that pretty yellow satchel, my dear? Did you bring me a present?" He tittered as he moved toward the satchel but stopped just short of snatching its strap. "Oh, that's right. Silly me. You didn't expect to find me here, did you? Still, I'm curious. Did you bring a little something for Judah?"

He was taunting me, but I made a silent vow to be civil.

"No, I just bought some toiletries for my maid," I answered while picturing the tablet inside the satchel, feeling its weight against my hip, and peeping at the strap dangling over the edge of the bench less than an arm's length from him. I lifted my chin and squared my shoulders, but his smirk told me he'd caught the lie anyway.

So I changed the subject.

"Did you know that instead of going to Jerusalem, my maid and I will be returning to Alexandria on the next merchantman? But I did want to thank you for your hospitality, both in your home, your shop, and—"

"My hospitality?" He forced out a bitter laugh and then broke it off abruptly. "Surely you're joking. You've been abusing my hospitality since Judah first brought you here, on a Shabbat no less. You're nothing but a common thief intent on getting your greedy hands on my recipe whether by stealing it outright, which you tried to do from the beginning—oh, no, I haven't forgotten the time you ransacked my study—and when that failed, you began nosing into how I acquired it. You're a resolute bitch all right, a curse on me and our people since you arrived here.

"Don't you know the only hope for Judean farmers losing their land to the likes of you rests in my having exclusive owner-ship of that recipe?" Here the timbre of his voice changed from a strident staccato to a crone's whine cracking with emotion. "That otherwise only bad times are ahead for our people? How dare you thank me for my hospitality, you, the very one seeking to destroy our people's only hope!

"And don't you know that because of you I accidentally killed a harmless old woman and brought tragedy to a pious Judean family?"

I couldn't believe it. He blamed me for her death.

"And because of you I had to kill your bloodsucking comrade from Alexandria?"

My G-d! Why is he telling me this?

"I saw the two of you with your heads together at the reception. Do you think I'm blind? He was telling you he sold me the recipe, wasn't he? And I'll bet you were trying to wheedle him into giving you—not even selling but giving you—a copy outright. I know your wiles."

His voice rumbled like thunder, but the word "wiles" flamed out like a savage cry. Still, it was his look that churned my blood, that demonic gleam in his eyes and his stain devouring that light.

"What? Is that what you think?" A shrill laugh seasoned with spite erupted from my innards. So much for my vow of civility. "Drakon could sell you the recipe—and for the fortune he must have demanded—because you were stupid enough to think you'd be his sole customer. The others weren't so foolish. They bought their copies by the armful."

I dug the tablet out of the satchel and thrust it under his nose.

Reeling with indignation, his stain blackening, he seized the tablet, squinting at it through the sweat dripping from his brow. As he wiped his face, a few strands of his wig got caught on one of the rings. And then with the sweep of his hand, the hairpiece itself wheeled through the air before landing like a dead pigeon in the *impluvium*. But his attention was focused elsewhere. Gawking at the tablet for a dense moment, he unleashed a chilling wail that rang through the atrium and then a bellow of rage that echoed through the house as if in pursuit of that wail.

In the instant that followed, he hurled the tablet whereupon it ricocheted against one of the ebony doors and smashed the *hydria* beside it to smithereens. After the clatter, I heard a hiss, and then a coppery-red Egyptian cobra about three feet long, probably bewildered by the unfamiliar light, undulated laterally through the wreckage before sidewinding toward the *triclinium* on the smooth marble floor.

"Now look at what you've done. You've disturbed my pet and destroyed my *hydria*." Spittle sputtered from his mouth with each crazed syllable.

I should have run from him then.

When I had the chance.

Out through the doors, down the peony-lined walkway, and into the street.

Instead, I just stood there, rooted by that luminescent birthmark as if its spreading darkness would engulf his entire face and make him disappear.

And then it was too late.

A glint of brass, and he pulled out a *sica*.

"I've looked forward to this moment since that first Shabbat when I realized you'd stop at nothing to get what you want." His eyes widened, and his lips curved in a triumphant smile. "I tried to kill you twice, you know, but now you're mine, and I promise to butcher you slowly."

He stood poised to strike.

I remembered what Binyamin taught me: *Watch his feet and measure his reach.*

Mine is longer.

I stretched out my arms and clawed his eyes before he could lunge.

He screamed, from rage or pain I could not tell.

His eyes watered.

But he moved in and shoved me back.

I slammed into the bench and grabbed the satchel by its strap.

Now I was Binyamin with the net.

I swung the satchel to whack the *sica* out of his hand.

Once.

Twice.

And then it clanged to the floor.

He dropped to one knee to retrieve it, but it has caromed too far.

I pulled at my skirts to kick him in the groin.

But he was on his feet in no time.

He balled his fists and landed a solid left hook and a straight overhand right.

The first grazed my mouth. The second wrapped me in coils of pain.

I tasted blood and swam through the nausea.

He seized the strap to rip it from my grip.

I let go.

Suddenly.

He skittered backward, tripping on the marble skirt of the *impluvium*, falling into the basin, scraping his head on its cobbled floor.

Spirals of blood tinged the water.

He scrambled out, soaking wet, breathing hard, sucking in air, a gash on the back of his head, his mouth drooling rills of spittle, his eyes bulging with fury.

"Now you die!"

I watched his feet.

And braced for his advance.

I sidestepped his punch.

Then pow! I planted a left hook on the side of his head.

And leaned back from his jab as he swung at the air.

I shot a glance at the snake.

In that split second, he hurtled into me.

I stumbled backward and fell to the floor.

The air exploded out of my lungs.

He pounced.

We rolled and twisted with the intimacy of lovers.

His birthmark, now a satiny black, consumed his face.

He bashed my head against the floor.

A siren of pain.

Another bash.

My teeth bit my tongue.

Aroused by the vibrations, the snake slithered toward us.

I tried to rake Eran's eyes, but his face was a blur.

He turned his head to avoid the clawing.

And saw the snake.

Approaching him.

Treacherously coiled.

Hood expanding.

He leaped to his feet and snatched the snake stick behind the remaining *hydria*.

While I seized the head of Apollo that caps it.

And slammed it against his shoulder blade.

The snap of bone, a ghastly howl, and he doubled over, crumpled to the floor, his eyes rolling back, and then nothing.

Resting Apollo's head on the floor, I picked up the snake stick, and, hovering behind the cobra, I slipped the hook around its neck just below the hood. Then, carrying its writhing body at arm's length, my head ringing, my legs wobbling against the weight of pain, I crossed the atrium and released the creature into the *hydria*. Finally, I lifted Apollo's head and heard the clack as its base fit into the neck of the jug.

I must have dropped the snake stick somewhere during my trudge to the bench because all I remembered was lying down and grasping my elbows to contain the shudders of relief.

And then I heard something.

Are those footsteps or only the shrieks of my pain?

Someone was coming.

A bar of light slanted toward me.

A hint of sandalwood or only a hallucination?

Judah rushing to my side.

While shouting to Eran.

The pain loosening its grip.

My consciousness ebbing.

"IS ERAN ALIVE?" I mumbled through the deep afternoon

shadows looming over me.

"Yes, he's beginning to moan. I have some tincture of opium. When I know I can leave you, I'll get it for him."

"I think I'll need some too. But what made you happen by?" I asked as I pressed my palms against the bench, rocked forward, and stood up with underwater slowness. "He told me you'd be in the shop until he relieved you."

"That's true, but he planned to drop by anyway on his way to the palace. He wanted to show me his designs before he brought them to Alexander. I knew he was keen on the appointment, so when it started getting late—"

"*Shhhh.* Did you hear something?"

It sounded like a *whoosh* of air.

Or an intake of breath.

Two figures draped in black emerged from the forest of lamp stands in the *triclinium*. They might have slipped in through a window. Who can say? But before another moment could unfold, they flowed across the atrium, their cloaks billowing like wings. Crouching on either side of Eran, they pulled him up by his elbows, whispered something to him in Aramaic, and lowered him back to the floor. Next one of them flashed his *sica*, straddled Eran, and behind the screen of his cloak, slashed Eran's throat.

Blood spurted out as if from a fountain.

The crimson pool widened slowly, radiating its ghastly rivulets.

A perfect copy of the symbol I thought was a radiant sun.

Next the men turned to Judah.

I froze in horror.

But they just looked at him with their dark, piercing eyes.

"Don't worry," said the huskier of the two. "We're not after you. We know who you are. Your brother killed our blessed mother. He was a great soldier for us, your brother, an ardent patriot with the ear of the procurator, but he became reckless, out of control, killing for his own purposes. We would have had to put him down for that alone, before he did any more harm and excited the notice of the authorities."

"And we know your brother also killed Alexander's scribe," said the other. "Good riddance, and may a similar fate befall the rest of them in that pestilential palace." The corner of his upper lip twisted in contempt. "We've claimed credit for that murder, so you needn't worry the authorities will drag you in for questioning. As far as the procurator is concerned, the case is closed."

With that, they turned as one and melted into the silent shadows of the *triclinium*.

Chapter 29

Late Friday Afternoon

THE LAST OF the minyan from Eran's synagogue had left, Jabin and the houseboys were preparing for Shabbat, and Judah and I were sitting opposite each other in a far corner of the *triclinium*. There the blooms of bowing peonies screened us from the clutter that dominated the rest of the room, but their fragrance could not discourage the flies or mask the stench of death.

"Judah, I hope you can take comfort from Eran's funeral, especially from the many farmers who came, each like a brother, to say *Kaddish* with you. Even the eulogy the procurator's representative delivered honored Eran as a master craftsman."

Judah was sitting forward in a bulky armchair, his body bent, his forearms across his thighs. His eyes had dropped to his lap, so all I saw of them was a fringe of lashes against his sallow complexion. Long golden pools of afternoon light gathered at his feet, but darkness engulfed him anyway.

I looked for any sign he could love me, even chastely, though I longed to taste the salty tang of his lips and open every other part of my being to him, if only but once. Could he have even a spark of desire for me after my bitter relationship with his brother? But I saw only a face numbed by the shock and sorrow of a sudden and bewildering calamity.

Still, whether or not he could love me, he was entitled to know what had brought me to Caesarea and why, even at the risk of antagonizing his brother, I kept pursuing the recipe. So, despite the elaborate stories budding in my throat, I resolved to tell the truth.

I gazed at him, and when he felt my look, his eyes met mine.

"Judah, about the League's scrolls? Remember the ones you lent me two years ago? And one of them had the recipe you and Saul were working on to perfect copper?" Every sentence was coming out like a question, so I took a deep breath to bolster my courage.

"Actually, the scrolls had been out of my possession for an entire week. Never mind why, but Noah filched all three of them. At the time, I didn't know where they were or if I could even get them back. That's why I lied and said I just forgot to bring them. I didn't want to alarm you, and I needed time to try to recover them."

I was too embarrassed to add that I was afraid he'd never take me seriously either as an alchemist or a woman if he knew I'd lost the scrolls.

"But that's not the worst of it. Unbeknownst to me, Drakon, who was Noah's scribe at the time, made copies of your recipe. Then, after Noah fired him, he sold them to not only your brother but at least a score of others throughout the Empire and beyond."

He listened calmly, relaxing into the chair, attending to my confession with nods and squints.

"When I got your letter last June, I wondered whether Eran could have gotten hold of your recipe. I couldn't imagine how, but needles of unease pricked my conscience anyway. After all, how many alchemists could have been working on the perfection of copper? So that's why I came here, to find out how Eran got his hands on the recipe and forestall the spread of its secrets."

There. My shoulders dropped as the relief spread through me.

I continued by explaining what I'd learned in Caesarea and ended by asking him to forgive me.

"Oh, Miriam, I knew at the time you were fibbing, that you are too methodical to have forgotten anything as important as the scrolls. I was annoyed, but I figured you had your reasons and sooner or later you'd return them. And you did.

"Another thing. Don't worry about Drakon's copies. The

directions are clear to us, but I doubt whether anyone outside the League can follow them. You know how technical, even cryptic, our jargon is. Besides, Saul warned me that no matter what, the particulars of our recipe would eventually fan out beyond the Seed of Abraham, that the economy was too desperate and gold too scarce to contain such a secret indefinitely."

Oh my G-d, was my whole trip here for naught? My lie and the cover-up as well?

"My issue is not with your lie but the lie I kept telling myself." Again, as his habit, he raked his hands through his hair. "As much as I denied it, I knew shortly after I met my brother that he was unbalanced and yes, dangerous. But as the favored son, I felt responsible for the hardships he faced growing up and for his leaving Alexandria and having to make his way without a father's guidance. So I made ever more elaborate excuses for him, hoping all the while I could stem his jealousy, even as he hated me."

"He hated you? I knew he hated me but—"

"He didn't hate you, Miriam; he was afraid of you. And when he was in the throes of his mania, he'd curse you for scheming to steal his recipe, for intending to use the gold you'd make to buy up the peasants' land."

He paused for a thoughtful moment. When he spoke again, his voice was thick with sorrow.

"No, Miriam, he railed against you because you were a part of my life. I'm the one he hated, the illegitimate brother who deprived him of all he ever wanted, a father's love. And he churned that deepest desire into the deadliest hate, that of a man for his brother."

"Oh, Judah. He was like a snail, trapped in a twisted shell but too vulnerable to escape."

In my weariness, I felt a twinge of pity for Eran, enough for my chin to tingle and a film of tears to sting my eyes. "Can we be grateful that at least he died quickly? After all, as a Judean patriot and freedom fighter, he could have faced a grisly public execution not just as Drakon's murderer but as a member of the notorious *Sicarii*."

"You're right, of course. And he had an honorable burial, the kind he'd have wanted. But he'd also have wanted his work to continue. So that's why I've decided to stay on. I'll need Jabin's help, of course, to liquidate Eran's estate, but as the sole heir, I can dedicate the assets to the Judean farmers, to help them pay their taxes and hold onto their land. And in the meantime, I'll run Eran's business. I think Saul would want me to take care of my brother this way, not just to say *Kaddish* for him but to perform *tzedakah*, righteous acts, in his name."

"But what about our work with the League?"

"You know, Miriam, I've lost interest since Saul's passing. But more to the point, you don't need me anymore for the members to accept you. You've more than proved your worth with your apparatus for condensing mercury vapors. I wouldn't be surprised if they ask you someday to work on the elixir to restore youth."

I felt my voice getting small, but I dared to ask him anyway.

"Does this mean I won't see you again?"

"Maybe."

"Oh."

That's all I said, just that one word. We could have spoken about so many things, but nothing else mattered anymore.

Epilogue

Alexandria, One Year Later

LIFE STRETCHES forward not backward. Since my return, I've learned to make a stable form of *acidum salis* by heating and distilling a mixture of salt and oil of vitriol (sulfuric acid). Aside from comparing samples of brass, I've used it to remove the rusty lace from the wrought iron furnishings in our courtyard. Imagine something as practical as that! And, as Judah predicted, the League has asked me to work on the elixir to heal, rejuvenate, and extend human life.

He's still in Caesarea. I don't hear from him, but I hear about him from the other jewelers in the synagogue. Just as he said he would, he's established a fund in Eran's memory to support the impoverished farmers in Judea. Sometimes I dream of him and see before me the contours of his body, his thick black curls, and his rugged cleft chin. But as soon as I open my eyes, the images float away, and I'm left with only a needlelike ache that is both painful and exquisite. Other times, especially when I'm working in the lab, I sense him guiding me in the practical matters of alloying metals. And occasionally, I even hear him reminding me to own up to my lies. In these ways, his presence sustains me.

I spend the rest of my time managing my father and Amram's business interests, expanding their assets beyond anything Noah could have imagined. He'd be so proud of me. Phoebe has taken charge of our household with the help of the additional servants I've purchased to care for Papa and Aunt Hannah, who've begun to show their age. Phoebe has an especially good day whenever she receives a letter from Bion, which is often.

Aunt Hannah once told me that when my mother felt life quicken inside her, she went to an astrologer who told her she'd have a daughter with great gifts but also great losses. I lost Noah, and now I wonder whether the Fates ordained that I'd also lose Judah. And I fear I may likewise lose Binyamin, who's achieved great fame in arenas as far away as Mérida (Spain), Périgueux (France), and Pompeii (Italy). I write to him regularly, but so far I've received only an occasional answer.

In closing, I can only hope this story of my lie and its consequences will serve as a lesson to others. In the meantime, I pray that the Almighty will forgive my part in the deaths of Eran, Drakon, and the Judean matron, that He will bring Binyamin home to me safely, and that He will continue to judge me worthy of His instruction in the Divine Art, all for His glory.

With gratitude toward Our Creator,

Μιριαμ βατ Ισααχ

The seal of Miriam bat Isaac
Alexandria *ad Aegyptum*
Summer of the Ninth Year of the Reign of Tiberius
Claudius Caesar Augustus Germanicus [Claudius]

Author's Note

Miriam bat Isaac is not entirely a figment of my imagination. I have based her life on the little that is known of the legendary founder of Alexandrian alchemy, the ardent Jewess (Patai, 1994) who held her place for 1500 years as the most celebrated woman of the Western World. In the alchemical literature, she is referred to as Maria Hebrea, Mary the Jewess, or Miriam the Prophetess, sister of Moses, but no one knows her real name. All alchemists wrote under the name of a deity, prophet, or philosopher from an earlier time perhaps to enhance the authenticity of their claims but certainly to shield themselves from persecution. Amid accusations of cheating their clients, destabilizing the currency, or worst yet, of financing the overthrow of the Empire, they could be arrested, tortured, and executed.

The persona for Maria Hebrea is invented, but the political context of Miriam bat Isaac's stay in Caesarea is historically accurate. Scholars (e.g., Korb, 2010; Rops, 1962; Smallwood, 1976) document the progressive breakdown of law and order throughout the early decades of first-century CE Judea in response to direct Roman rule: the underground resistance of the Zealots, whether by guerilla warfare or agricultural strikes; the pseudo-messiahs and false prophets; and the urban cells of the *Sicarii*, who directed their terrorist attacks against individuals they deemed faithless and treacherous. Yet, despite the tens of thousands of crucifixions and the class divisions among the Jews themselves, the procurators were only partially and temporarily successful in suppressing the uprisings and revolts.

Other particulars incorporated into the story are less certain. For example, I repeat the story Hopkins (1985) tells of Claudius, that when the equipment to hoist animals into the arena failed, he ordered the stage mechanics to fight in the animals' place. Inasmuch as Hopkins does not report when this event took place, it could have occurred anytime during Claudius's reign (41 to 54 CE), even shortly after the time of my story.

For another example, Holum et al. (1988), Lewin (2005), and Levine (1975) each refer to the hippodrome that Herod built as being outside and to the east of the city walls (to protect the city from the ribald crowds). Netzer (2006) on the other hand puts Caesarea's hippodrome inside the city walls adjacent to the Upper Palace. I've set Alexander's gladiatorial games in Netzer's location, but in case there was more than one sports amphitheater, I have called the site next to the palace a stadium rather than a hippodrome. My description of its arena, tiers of seats, *hypogeum*, and ceremonies is based on Quennell's (1971) account of the Colosseum built about thirty years after my story. Seeing that the stadiums and rituals evolved with time and place, I cannot be sure of their accuracy for 48 CE Caesarea.

Scholars also differ as to whether Maria Hebrea discovered *acidum salis*, known centuries later as hydrochloric acid. According to the *Encyclopaedia Judaica* ("Alchemy," 2007), she was "the first to mention hydrochloric acid and one may therefore assume that she discovered it" (p. 602). But according to Leicester (1971), hydrochloric acid was not discovered until the thirteenth century and not prepared until the sixteenth century. Other sources, however, say Maria Hebrea *probably* discovered it. For the sake of the story, I have Miriam using hydrochloric acid as a digestive aid (as it is sometimes used today), although I could find no references to it in the literature on ancient medicine (e.g., Kelly, 2009).

And no one is certain about some of the city's landmarks. Scholars agree that as a Roman city, Caesarea must have had a forum, but where was it? Some locate a forum east of the Temple of Augustus and Roma (Netzer, 2006). More in accord with Holum et al. (1988), I have located the Forum approximately midway between the harbor and each of the city's three gates. Likewise I have elaborated beyond the hypothetical details Netzer (2006) provides for the Temple of Augustus and Roma to adorn it with a rose garden, tessellated floor, and coffered ceiling.

Finally, on perhaps a less substantial matter, scholars differ on how the thumb was turned to signal the fate of a fallen gladiator. Quennell (1971) claims an upturned thumb meant his life was to be spared; a downward thumb, he was to be killed on the spot. Hopkins (1985), however, claims only that the thumb was turned. If not downward, then it might have been turned upward or sideways. And according to Shadrake (2005), the thumb was turned outward to signal death. To allow for these alternative views, I had the spectators' and Alexander's thumbs simply turn.

Thus, although the story along with most of its characters is fiction, it is based on the research of scholars. Here are some of the sources I've relied on:

Alchemy. (2007). In *Encyclopaedia Judaica* (2nd. ed.). (Vol. 1, p. 602). Farmington Hills, MI: Macmillan Reference USA.

Casson, L. (1971). *Ships and seamanship in the Ancient World.* Princeton, NJ: Princeton University Press.

Casson, L. (1994). *Travel in the Ancient World.* Baltimore, MD: Johns Hopkins University Press.

Holmyard, E. J. (1957). *Alchemy.* Baltimore, MD: Penguin Books.

Holum, K. G., Hohlfelder, R. L., Bull, R. J., & Raban, A. (1988). *King Herod's Dream: Caesarea on the Sea.* New York: W. W. Norton.

Hopkins, K. (1985). Murderous games. In *Death and renewal: Sociological studies in Roman history* (Vol. 2, pp. 1-30). New York: Cambridge University Press.

Houston, M. G. (1931). *Ancient Greek, Roman, and Byzantine costume and decoration.* London: A. & C. Black.

Jashemski, W. F. (1993). *The gardens of Pompeii: Herculaneum and the villas destroyed by Vesuvius* (Vol. 2). New Rochelle, NY: Aristide D. Caratzas.

Kelly, K. (2009). *The history of medicine: Early civilizations, prehistoric times to 500 CE.* New York: Facts on File.

Korb, S. (2010). *Life in Year One: What the world was like in first-century Palestine.* New York: Riverhead Books.

Le Toquin, A., & Bosser, J. (2006). *Gardens in time.* New York: Harry N. Abrams.

Leicester, H. M. (1971). *The historical background of chemistry.* New York: Dover.

Levine, L. I. (1975). *Caesarea under Roman Rule.* Leiden, the Netherlands: E. J. Brill.

Lewin, A. (2005). *The archeology of Ancient Judea and Palestine.* Los Angeles: J. Paul Getty Museum.

Meijer, F. (2004). *The gladiators: History's most deadly sport.* (L. Waters, Trans.). New York: St. Martin's Press.

Netzer, E. (2006). *The architecture of Herod, the great builder.* Tübingen, Germany: Mohr Siebeck.

Patai, R. (1994). *The Jewish alchemists: A history and source book.* Princeton, NJ: Princeton University Press.

Quennell, P. (1971). *The Colosseum.* New York: Newsweek.

Rops, H. D. (1962). *Daily life in Palestine at the time of Christ.* (P. O'Brian, Trans.). London: Phoenix Press.

Shadrake, S. (2005). *The world of the gladiator.* Stroud, Gloucestershire, UK: Tempus Publishing Ltd.

Sly, D. I. (1996). *Philo's Alexandria.* London: Routledge.

Smallwood, E. M. (1976). *The Jews under Roman Rule: From Pompey to Diocletian.* Leiden, the Netherlands: E. J. Brill.

Vann, R. L. (1991). The Drusion: A candidate for Herod's lighthouse at Caesarea Maritima. *The International Journal of Nautical Archeology, 20*(2), 123-139.

Aside from the authors of these texts and the many friends who have cheered for me, especially Professor Jean Lythcott, my inspiration, I'm grateful to Professor Lewis M. Greenberg, an expert on ancient art and culture, and Dr. Bonnie M. Kaye, a psychologist with such an intuitive sense of people, for their encouragement and criticism as they waded through earlier drafts of this story.

Most of all, I am grateful to my husband, Paul R. Zuckerman, for his enduring love and unabashed pride in and promotion of my work.

Glossary of Foreign Terms

acidum salis (Latin) an early name for hydrochloric acid, produced from common salt and vitriol (sulfuric acid)

ad Aegyptum (Latin) literally "by Egypt," meaning that Alexandria was not considered part of the Roman province of Egypt. Instead Alexandria belonged to only the Emperor.

agoranomoi (Greek) market inspectors elected to set prices for certain goods, certify the accuracy of weights and scales, and control the exchange of currency

auctoratus (Latin) a hired gladiator, trained and obligated by contract to perform for a specified period of time

balnea (Latin) a small, privately owned bathhouse; **balneae** (pl.)

balneatricis (Latin) bath attendants

bellum justum (Latin) a just war

bestiarii (Latin) the gladiators trained to fight wild animals in the arena

bibliopōleion (Greek) bookshop

bisellium (Latin) ordinarily a seat for two people but referring here to the wide, cushioned, ornate chair for the procurator in the center of his *tribunal.*

calamistrum (Latin) curling iron

calamus (Latin) a pen made from bronze or more commonly from a reed cut at an angle and then split; **calami** (pl.)

calcei (Latin) shoes worn outdoors; had covered toes and straps extending to the ankles, calves, or knees

caldarium (Latin) the hottest room of the Roman baths

capitium (Latin) a short, light chemise used as a woman's undergarment or for sleeping

cardo (Latin) a north-south running street in a Roman city or military camp; **cardines** (pl.)

Cardo Maximus (Latin) the main north-south thoroughfare in a Roman city or military camp

cella (Latin) a garret room or mean apartment

coactoris (Latin) money collectors

colobium (Latin) a coarse, short-sleeved, workingman's tunic

corbita (Latin) literally a "basket" but refers here to a wide sailing ship with a rounded, big-bellied hull for cargo

cubiculum (Latin) a sleeping chamber

damnatio ad bestia (Latin) literally "condemnation to beasts," refers to a form of public execution for common criminals in which the condemned was thrown to the wild beasts

decumanus (Latin) an east-west running street in a Roman city or military camp; **decumani** (pl.)

Decumanus Maximus (Latin) the main east-west thorough-fare in a Roman city or military camp

dulcia domestica (Latin) a chilled dessert made from pitted dates soaked in wine and stuffed with dried fruit, nuts, cake crumbs, and spices

exomis (Greek) a short, left-sleeved, laborer's tunic that bares the right half of the wearer's chest

frigidarium (Latin) the coldest room of the Roman baths

Hoc Habet! (Latin) the savage cry of spectators at the games meaning "Now he's had it!"

horrea (Latin) storehouses, e.g., granaries

hospita (Latin) an innkeeper, generally a woman

hydria (Latin) an ornamental water jug; **hydriae** (pl.)

hypogeum (Greek) literally "underground" but refers here to the vast network of cells, chambers, and tunnels below the arena

impluvium (Latin) the shallow sunken pool in the floor of an atrium, receives rainwater coming through the opening in the roof above it

instita (Latin) a Roman-style border or flounce on a lady's tunic

Kaddish (Aramaic) a prayer in praise of G-d that is recited in the company of a minyan. Referring here specifically to the Mourner's *Kaddish*, the prayer is recited for thirty days after the death of a child, spouse, or sibling; for eleven months after the death of a parent; and again at every anniversary of the death.

kapēleion (Greek) a snack bar providing cold snacks and beverages

laena (Latin) a round cloak to cover the shoulders

ludus (Latin) a school to train gladiators

murmillo (Latin) a type of gladiator armed with a long sword, large shield, and visored helmet

navis oneraria (Latin) a ship of burden, built to carry cargo

pedisequi (Latin) the slaves who accompany a litter to secure its safety, one duty being to part the crowds so as to make way for the porters

pompa (Latin) the colorful parade during which the gladiators enter the arena

Porta Triumphalis (Latin) literally "Gate of Triumph," refers to one of the two main gates that led into the arena in Caesarea's stadium, specifically the gate for those who would be participating in an athletic competition or military ceremony

praegenarii (Latin) the dwarfed, crippled, and/or deformed men who, using wooden weapons, mimic the gladiators to amuse the crowd

primus palus (Latin) literally "the first pole," the title given to the best combatants within a *ludus*

puer (Latin) boy servant, bellboy

retiarius (Latin) the only type of gladiator to fight without a helmet, specialized in using a net and trident as his weaponry, trained to fight a *secutor*

Roma (Latin) the goddess personifying the city of Rome and the Roman state

saniarium (Latin) the chamber where wounded gladiators are taken for medical treatment

Sebastos (Greek) translates as "venerable one" in English or "augustus" in Latin. Herod the Great chose this name for his harbor to honor his emperor.

secutor (Latin) the type of gladiator armed with only a short sword, trained to fight a *retiarius*

Shabbat (Hebrew) the Sabbath, the seventh day of the Jewish week, a day of rest observed from a few minutes before sunset on Friday to a few minutes after three stars appear in the sky on Saturday night

sica (Latin) a short, curved dagger used by the *Sicarii* and the type of gladiator known as a *thraex*; **sicae** (pl.)

Sicarii (Latin) a secret brotherhood of assassins named for the short daggers, the **sicae**, they concealed under their cloaks

Sicarius (Latin) an assassin belonging to the secret brotherhood

soleae (Latin) sandals, footwear with open toes, worn indoors by both men and women

Soteria (Greek) literally "the Savior," refers to the Greek goddess of safety, preservation, and deliverance

spoliarium (Latin) the pit below the arena where the bodies of slain beasts and gladiators are dumped to await mass burial

stationes (Latin) the offices shippers maintained in major commercial centers to promote their business

strigilis (Latin) a curved instrument of metal or bone used in the baths to scrape away dead skin

strophium (Latin) a band women wore over their tunic and under their bust to support their breasts

summum supplicium (Latin) the most extreme punishment

synthesis (Latin) a loose gown the host wore at dinner parties

tepidarium (Latin) the warm room of the Roman bath

thermopolium (Latin) a Roman-style cookshop or fast-food café serving both hot and cold foods

thraex (Latin) a type of gladiator armed with a *sica*; a small, almost square shield; and a visored helmet

tonsor (Latin) a barber

Torah (Hebrew) the *Pentateuch*, the Five Books of Moses, the foundation of all Jewish legal and ethical precepts

tribunal (Latin) a raised platform for seating dignitaries

triclinium (Latin) a Roman dining room, also used for entertaining

tunica interior (Latin) the fitted undergarment a woman wore under her outer tunic (*tunica exterior*)

tzedakah (Hebrew) literally means "righteousness" but commonly refers to the religious obligation to perform charitable acts

Verbera! (Latin) Strike!

Early Roman Emperors

Name—Reign

Augustus—27 BCE to 14 CE

Tiberius—14 CE to 37 CE

Caligula—37 CE to 41 CE

Claudius—41 CE to 54 CE

About the Author

With an EdD in science education, June Trop (Zuckerman) has focused her recent research on the mentoring of novice teachers, their classroom management strategies, and the practical knowledge they construct and communicate through storytelling. She is an associate professor emerita at the State University of New York at New Paltz.

55671420R00115